THE
PROMISE

THE PROMISE

CHANDRA SPARKS TAYLOR

Recycling programs
for this product may
not exist in your area.

THE PROMISE

ISBN-13: 978-0-373-83144-9

© 2010 by Chandra Sparks Taylor

www.KimaniTRU.com

Printed in U.S.A.

To my brothers, Andra Donell Sparks and Cedric DeJuan Sparks Sr. Thanks for showing me the importance of family and for your unwavering love and support. I hope I've made you as proud of me as I am of you and that I've shown the world I'm from a good neighborhood.

In loving memory of my granddaddy, Reverend George Jones Sr., and my cousin, Jocelyn Jones Stewart. I love you and I miss you.

Acknowledgments

Once again I am humbled to pen my acknowledgments. First and foremost, to God who continues to open doors no man can open and who is the center of my joy. Thank you for allowing my wildest dream to come true—again. In all I do and say, I pray I am sharing your power with the next generation, your mighty miracles to all who are to come.

To my Jessica—my girl for life. Thank you for continuing to be the light of my life. My best days without you don't compare to my worst days with you. I am so thankful to be your mommy. Always know how much I love you and how proud I am of you.

To my family: my parents, the late Cedric Sparks and the late Doris Jones Sparks; my brothers, Andra and Cedric; my sisters-in-law, Karen and Pamela; my nieces and nephews, Anthony, Brittany, Cedric Jr., DeJa, and Chancellor; Jamaal Taylor; my uncle Edward Johnson (and Arianna and Sally); my grandparents Lela Mae Jones, the late George Jones Sr., and the late Ida B. Sparks; and my great-aunt, Rosie Mae O'Bryant; my aunts, Carolyn Jones Hollman and Geraldine Jones Murray as well as the rest of my extended family. I love you.

To my girls, Toni Staton Harris and Allilsa Bradley. Thank you for always having my back and for being my true friends. You are the sisters I never had, and I love you dearly. Thanks also to Angela Coppins, Clem and Claudette Richardson, Jacquelin Thomas, Lisa Kimble, Lisa Jones, Mr. and Mrs. Charles McCafferty and Tamala Maddox.

I must acknowledge my church families: Forty-fifth Street Baptist Church, First Missionary Baptist Church, East Boyles, and Shiloh Baptist Church.

I would be remiss if I didn't acknowledge the staff at A.G. Gaston Elementary School, especially Fred Stewart, Terry Bush, Kristi Cunningham (hey, Shannon!), Venita Grimmett, Alike Johnson, Melonie Pippins, Andrea Cockrell, Donna McCollum, Willie Brown, Kimberly Hudson, Bessie Taylor, Mr. Paul, Mrs. Eula, Ms. Abbott and Carol Biggs. I must also mention my students: Brooke, TaMarcus, Devonta, Donterrious, Jeremiah, Rishard, Andria, Le'Shaureah, TeAni, Tanaysha, Breyonna, Briana, Tameria and Jayla. Thank you for embracing me and for your patience as I learned the teaching ropes. If I've forgotten anyone, please charge it to my head and not my heart.

To all the libraries, schools, organizations and conferences who have been so supportive of me, especially the Birmingham Public Libraries, Denise Allen, Maya Jones, Deborah Holloway, Velister Debro, Linda Cox, Rosemary Thomas and Beverly Brown. Thank you.

To the media, especially Chanda Temple Guster, Joey Kennedy and Janet Fink and the University of Alabama Alumni magazine, NBC 13, ABC 33/40 and Birmingham Public Library for their coverage.

To Glenda Howard and the staff of Kimani Press for your continued faith in me as well as Stacy Luecker, Regina Waller, Kris White, Charles Ghigna, Leah Wiggins, Little Professor Bookstore and Jac'Quese Smith for your assistance.

Finally, to the readers who continue to be so supportive and enthusiastic. Thank you for once again being a part of my dream. I pray *The Promise* shows you the importance of family and friends and that we have the opportunity to meet soon. Until next time, may your wildest dreams come true.

one

squeaking sneakers and the hustle and flow of the basketball players across the gymnasium floor charged me as I waved my arms, signaling I was open so my teammate could pass me the ball.

She bounced it to me, and I snatched it before focusing on the goal and sinking it in for three points. Nothing but net.

It was the final game of the summer basketball league's season, and I was giving it my all. Since deciding at the end of my junior year to give up my spot as cheerleading cocaptain to play ball, I had thrown myself into each game. I had learned a lot over the summer, both about basketball and myself, and I was looking forward to my senior year, which was only a few weeks away.

Coach Miller called a time-out with only three minutes left in the game, and I jogged off the court, glancing up into the stands when I heard my dad yell, "Go, Courtland."

He had been at all my games along with my mom, my nine-year-old sister Cory, my best friend, Sabrina Davis, and a few members of my purity group, Worth the Wait. Knowing I had so much support had me feeling better than I had in all my seventeen years.

Coach went over our final play, then my teammates and I gathered in a huddle, pumping each other up before we went back to the court and played to win. When it was all over, we'd lost by one point, but I was grinning like we had won the NBA championship.

I guzzled down a cup of Gatorade before going to congratulate the other team. As I was heading to the locker room, one of our opponents stopped me.

"Aren't you that girl who pressed charges against Allen Benson?" she asked, squinting at me from behind a pair of sports goggles.

I groaned inwardly. It had been a couple of days since someone had last asked me about Allen, my ex-boyfriend who was rumored to be joining a pro basketball team at the end of last school year.

Allen was fine and charming. He was my first boyfriend, and I loved him. I thought he loved me, too—until I snuck out to meet him one night. Not only had he tried to force himself on me, but he had also admitted he'd started dating me so he could get me to sleep with him to win a ten-dollar bet that he'd be the one to make me lose my virginity.

He had done a lot of messed-up things while we were together—putting his hands on me, and fooling around with other girls, one of whom was also pressing charges. I'm not sure who the girl was, but it was rumored that she was from a political family.

It wasn't until after my aunt Loretta Danielle Dennis ended up in the hospital that I learned he'd been seeing her, too. She claimed she was pregnant by him, and he'd gotten so mad during their argument that he'd run over her with his car. Allen claimed it was an accident, but I saw the video my sister, Cory, had managed to shoot that night, and I believe it was intentional.

I finally decided to press charges against Allen for what he had done to me after my little sister, Cory, witnessed what he did to Aunt Dani. I felt as though I had to set a good example for Cory and not let Allen get away with what he'd tried to do to me, but I had changed my mind about a month ago. I just wanted to move on with my life.

My charges had been the least of Allen's worries. He was also being investigated by the NBA for accusations he'd accepted gifts from two coaches.

"Well, are you?" the girl repeated, using a forearm to wipe a trail of sweat from her forehead. I briefly wondered why she was sweating so much since she had been riding the bench the whole game.

A couple of her teammates gathered around waiting to hear my answer. I opened my mouth to speak, but before I could, Daddy rushed over and wrapped me in a bear hug.

"Good job, Courtland. I'm proud of you," he said.

He slung his arm around my shoulders and led me away from the girls, and I smiled. Mostly I was glad he had rescued me, but I also had to admit that it felt good to get a hug from my daddy and hear he was proud. It had been a while since he had done it, but it was starting to happen more often.

"You okay?" he whispered as we walked over to where Momma and Cory were waiting.

"Yes," I said. "Thanks for saving me."

Daddy and I had come a long way in the last few months—our whole family had. Daddy had finally admitted he was an alcoholic, and he was attending AA meetings every week. He was going to church with us, and he and Momma, who had never gotten married, were planning a big wedding for the Saturday of Labor Day weekend, the weekend before school started. Momma was so excited she was getting the wedding of which she had always dreamed, and so was I.

"You hungry?" Momma asked after congratulating me on a good game.

"Yep," I said before turning to my little sister. "Hey, munchkin."

"Hey," she said, frowning at my use of the nickname she now hated. "Can we go to Applebee's?"

"You're reading my mind," I said, already tasting the steak and shrimp parmesan and blondie dessert I was going to order.

"We'll walk over. I snuck out during the game and put

our names on the waiting list. They'll probably be calling us soon," Momma said. "You can head over once you get dressed."

Our game was at Fair Park Arena in Birmingham, Alabama, and we'd had a nice turnout. I knew a lot of people were probably going to be headed to Applebee's, which was right across the street, so I was glad Momma had thought ahead.

"Do you want me to wait for you?" Daddy asked, looking worried as he glanced around the almost empty arena.

"I'll be fine," I said. I tried to be casual about looking around to see if the girls who had asked me about Allen were still there, but Momma busted me.

"You sure?" she asked.

"You're treating her like a baby," Cory said, and I smiled my thanks.

They all watched me head toward the locker room to make sure I got there safely, then I watched them walk over to one of Daddy's police-officer friends.

I didn't hear what Daddy was saying, but I was sure he was telling him to keep an eye on me.

I was in and out of the locker room in fifteen minutes. As I headed for the exit, a girl waddling past caught my attention.

"Emily?" I said.

Emily Arrington was a cheerleader for our rivals, the Baldwin Eagles. She had also come to a few Worth the Wait meetings, but that had been months ago. She was a white girl, but she had plenty of booty, and she didn't mind shaking it.

My eyes widened when she turned around. I was pretty sure that wasn't a basketball she was sporting under her shirt.

"Hey, Courtland," she said, sounding tired. She rubbed her stomach, and I found myself feeling sorry for her.

"How are you?" I asked. I thought about saying congratulations, but I wasn't sure if that was the right thing to say to an unwed mother. I glanced at her ring finger to make sure she hadn't gotten married since the last time I saw her, but it was bare, and it looked like there had never been a ring on it.

"Sick all the time," she said. "Every time I turn around I'm throwing up."

I nodded sympathetically. "When are you due?" I asked.

"October 25," she said.

I calculated and realized she was about six months pregnant, which meant she'd been pregnant at the last Worth the Wait meeting she'd attended. She had been talking all this craziness about having a baby before she got married so she'd be able to hold on to the guy forever. I guess she had gotten her wish.

I adjusted my gym bag, trying to think of something else to say.

"How are things with Worth the Wait?" she asked.

"Good." I filled her in on the purity conference, which would end with a ball we were planning for the spring. Fathers and daughters were both going to take an oath, promising to be pure in thought and deed. Our Worth the Wait adviser, Andrea Mitchell, had read about the ball online, and most of our members loved the idea. It would give us a chance to dress up and have some fun.

After I was elected president of our chapter, I had come up with the idea to do an entire conference, hoping we would get some new members.

A cell phone rang, and Emily and I each glanced at ours, which meant we both had Beyoncé's latest hit as our ring tone.

A big smile broke across Emily's face, and she snapped open her phone.

"Hey, baby," she said, sounding like a contented cat. She talked for a few minutes, and I figured it was the perfect chance for me to get away and meet up with my family. I had just put one foot out the door when Emily's words stopped me. "I'll see you later tonight. I love you, Allen."

two

I couldn't even enjoy my steak and shrimp parmesan at Applebee's because I was so busy thinking about Allen and Emily.

There were a million questions racing through my mind. Was Emily really talking to Allen—my Allen? That raised the question of whether he ever really was mine.

If she was talking to Allen Benson, was she carrying his baby? I thought back to what had happened last school year. It was rumored a girl who had accused Allen of rape was pregnant. Was Emily that girl? If so, why would she start seeing him?

I finally decided to get a to-go box for my food.

"You okay?" Momma asked, looking at me strangely when I turned down dessert.

I nodded and took a sip of my watery soda.

"I didn't get a chance to tell you that someone from the Harbert Center called and said there was a cancellation, so we have it for the reception." Momma looked as though she was about to bounce out of her seat in the booth, she was so excited.

"That's great, Momma," I said, mustering a smile.

She pulled a notebook from her purse and jotted something down. "I'm glad the summer basketball season is over. I'm going to need your help. We only have about a month left before the wedding, and we still haven't picked out your dress."

"We can go tomorrow," I said without really thinking. Cory stopped playing with her Game Boy long enough to kick me under the table. I had promised her I would hang out with her the next day. I had been so busy with practices and games all summer that I really hadn't spent much time with my little sister, which I had been trying to do more of.

I looked at her, silently telling her I was sorry.

"We can make it a girls-only day," Momma said then turned to look at Daddy. "You have to work tomorrow, right, Corwin?"

"Yes," Daddy said, his gaze never leaving ESPN, which was playing on the television in the bar.

"We can be at David's Bridal when it opens," Momma said.

I groaned to myself. That meant that I wouldn't be sleeping late, and since Momma was in total wedding mode, we probably wouldn't get home until late the next evening. So much for a relaxing Saturday.

I didn't sleep well that night, thinking about Allen and Emily. As much as I tried to tell myself not to be bothered by it, I was. I knew he had been cheating on me, but I was still finding it hard to believe he was doing it with people right under my nose. Emily was bad enough, but my aunt Dani was worse. She had told Allen she was pregnant, too, but it turned out she was lying.

I found myself thinking back on all the time Allen and I had spent together. I mean, we were always together, but for him it had all been a joke. I couldn't believe he had been faking his feelings for me, all for a lousy ten dollars.

I woke up the next morning in a bad mood, and the last thing I wanted to do was spend the day looking at bridesmaids' dresses and talking about weddings. I threw on some jeans, a Worth the Wait T-shirt and my Air Force Ones and headed down for breakfast. Momma was in a really good mood and had cooked all Daddy's favorites: sausages, home fries, cheese eggs and pancakes. I helped myself to a little of everything, making a mental note I needed to start cutting back since the basketball season was over. I was planning to try out for the school basketball team, but until then, I really wasn't going to be exercising as much since I had quit the cheerleading squad. The last thing I wanted to do was put back on the twenty pounds I had taken off the summer before freshman year.

After we said grace, Momma got busy working on her wedding list and Cory shoveled down her food so she could become engrossed in her Game Boy as usual, so I didn't have to worry about making conversation, but the silence started getting to me. "Where's Daddy?" I asked.

"He already left," Momma said, not looking up from her list. "Remind me to stop by the Dollar Tree to buy some of those little bottles of bubbles for the reception."

I wanted to roll my eyes. What was the point of her making a list if she was just going to ask me to remind her of things?

"Did you decide what color we're going to wear?" I asked.

Cory and I were both going to be bridesmaids along with Momma's best friend from high school who used to be my cheerleading coach. I hadn't seen her since she had moved to another state right before my junior year, and I was glad because she had told everyone that the only reason I made the squad was because she and Momma were friends.

"I'm still trying to decide," Momma said. "It might just depend on what dresses I like."

"What else do we have to do today?" I asked.

Momma rattled off a list of things, and, as I'd expected, it looked like it was going to be an all-day event.

"Can I just follow you to David's Bridal? I promised Cory I would spend some time with her today, and you really don't need us for that other stuff."

I knew she was going to say no, but I figured it was worth a try.

"I really need your help," she said. "I didn't realize all that went into planning a wedding. It's giving me practice for when you girls get married, though." She smiled at me, and I fought the urge to say, *Like that will ever happen.*

Instead, I stood from the table, grabbed my empty plate and placed it in the sink.

"Is that what you're wearing?" Momma asked, frowning.

I looked down at my clothes. "Yes. What's wrong with it?"

"Don't you need to wear some heels to try on with your dress?"

"Momma, you want me to walk around all day in heels?" I complained.

"You do it all day at school."

"That's different," I said, not able to think of anything else to say.

I finally talked her into letting me keep on my sneakers and just taking the heels with me.

David's Bridal hadn't even opened by the time we made it there. I caught Cory gazing at Toys R Us, which was a few doors down, and I knew she was going to figure out a way to get a new video game out of the deal. I saw Momma eyeing LifeWay Christian Bookstore, and it made me realize I'd forgotten to bring a book with me. It had been a while since I'd read a good one, but I had been seeing a bunch of them for kids my age in Wal-Mart and at the West End Library lately, and my best friend, Sabrina Davis, had been talking about them nonstop for months, so I figured I'd read one.

When David's finally opened, we almost got trampled by all the women trying to get inside. I looked around in amazement, wondering where they'd all come from since the parking lot had looked really empty. Momma, Cory and I headed to the bridesmaids' section, and Momma immediately reached for this countrified gown. It was red with big white polka dots all over it and the skirt looked wide enough for me to hide Cory and about three other kids underneath.

"What do you think?" Momma asked.

I just looked at her and shook my head.

"What?" she said. "You don't like it?"

I watched her, trying to see if she was serious and relief filled me when I saw her crack the slightest smile.

"You had me worried for a minute," I said. "I thought you were losing taste in your old age, or maybe you just wanted to make sure you were the best-looking one at your wedding."

"Old?" Momma said.

We laughed and continued looking through the dresses, finally deciding on a lavender one for me. I really wanted strapless, but Momma wasn't having it, so we settled for one with spaghetti straps. I liked the way it flowed and imagined myself walking down the aisle to my future husband. When Allen's face popped into my head, I jumped a little, not believing I was still thinking about him after all he'd done.

"You want to go look for your dress now?" I asked Momma, who was trying to talk Cory into actually trying on the dress she had picked out for her. My little sister didn't wear dresses often, and although the dress Momma had chosen was cute, I knew Cory was going to complain that it made her itch, even if it wasn't true. It was like she was allergic to dresses. I couldn't really blame her. I had gone through my antidress phase, too. Even now, I only wore them on special occasions. Momma had stopped making us wear skirts and dresses to church when she realized it wasn't as big a deal anymore as it was when she was growing up.

At the mention of a dress for her, Momma beamed and forgot all about her conversation with Cory, who looked relieved to have the spotlight off her. She parked herself in a chair that someone was just vacating right outside the fitting room, and we piled all the stuff we had gathered on her before heading to the brides' dresses.

Momma spent about an hour looking at all the different styles before she finally settled on about five of them. The place seemed to be even more crowded, if that was possible, so we waited half an hour just to get a fitting room. It didn't take Momma long to try on four of the dresses. She was really discouraged because none of them looked right or was "the dress," as she described it. When she tried on the last one, our eyes met in the mirror and we grinned at each other and started jumping around like we were in fifth grade.

"This is it," she said.

I had to agree. The dress was off-white with sleeves

that fell slightly off the shoulders. There were tiny flowers around the fitted waist and full skirt, and Momma really did look like a princess.

"You look beautiful, Momma," I said.

"I feel beautiful," she admitted. "I haven't felt this beautiful in a long time."

She stood admiring herself in the dress for a few more minutes before Cory interrupted us.

"I'm hungry," she complained.

I looked at my watch and realized it was almost noon, and my stomach growled as if it knew what I was thinking.

Momma laughed. "Okay, okay, I get the hint," she said, slipping out of the dress. "You girls still need to try on yours."

Cory widened her eyes, looking as scared as she did whenever Momma told her she had to go to the dentist, and I felt a little sorry for her.

"It's not that bad," I said. "Once we're done in here, maybe Momma will take you to Toys R Us."

Cory immediately started grinning, and Momma just shook her head.

"Fine," she said. "I can't believe my own children are trying to bribe me."

An hour later, we were sitting in the middle of the Galleria, chilling over lunch. Cory had gobbled down her food and was really into her new video game, and Momma had her head stuck in her wedding notebook, muttering something about ordering napkins. I was just checking people out, trying to see if there was anyone I knew hanging out.

I was just about to ask if I could go into Forever 21 when I spotted this fine guy. He looked about six-two, and he was the color of caramel. I gulped when I felt my mouth start to water. I tried to keep myself from staring, which was easy for me to do when I saw the girl next to him. She hit him on the arm and started laughing at something he said. I found myself wondering if they were happy—really happy. Allen and I had gone to the mall together a couple of times, and I wondered if that's the way we looked to other people, happy and in love.

I shook my head, determined not to think of Allen anymore.

"Momma, I'm going into Forever 21. I'll be right back," I said. She nodded absently, and I just shook my head. I dumped the trash from my lunch then headed into the store, stopping right inside the door when I spotted a really cute outfit that would be perfect for the first day of school.

I looked around the store, eyeing a few more outfits I liked, before coming back to the first one. It was really just a pair of pants and a top, but something about it was different than any other outfit I owned. I figured it was mature, yet sexy, which was exactly the image I wanted to portray for my senior year. Before I could stop myself, I found myself in the dressing room trying the outfit on. It looked even better on me. The black pants were tight, but not so tight they had me looking nasty, and the black-white-and-fuchsia top was fitting me in all the right places. I came out so I could look in the three-way mirror, and I was sold. Now I just had to talk Momma into it.

"That looks really good on you," someone said from behind me.

I looked in the mirror and realized it was the girl I had seen in the mall with her fine boyfriend. "Thanks," I said, admiring the dress she was trying on. "Yours looks nice, too."

"Could you help me with the zipper?" she said, turning so her back was to me. "I would ask my brother, but I didn't want to walk through the store with my clothes all unzipped."

"That fine boy was your brother?" I asked and blushed. I didn't know if I was embarrassed that I had actually spoken what I was thinking or if it was relief that the guy wasn't her boyfriend.

She laughed. "Aidan always gets that reaction. We just moved here from Atlanta, and he and his girlfriend broke up, so he's free. Do you want me to introduce you?" she asked, glancing over her shoulder as I zipped her up. "He's a really nice guy, and I'm not just saying that because he's my twin."

As much as I wanted to say yes, I ended up shaking my head. I wasn't ready to get into another relationship. "That's okay," I said.

"You sure?" she asked, looking at me curiously.

"Yeah."

She shrugged and walked over to stand in front of the three-way mirror. The dress she had on looked really good on her, but she didn't seem to be convinced.

"Are you going to get it?" I found myself asking.

She shook her head. "I think it's a bit much for the first day of school. I don't know how kids dress at Grover, but at my school in Atlanta, this would be considered overkill."

"Did you say Grover?" I asked.

She nodded.

"That's where I go," I said.

She turned around and looked at me. "Are you serious?" she said. "Wait until I tell Aidan. I'm Nadia Calhoun, by the way."

"Courtland Murphy," I said, extending my hand so she could shake it. We stood there awkwardly for a few seconds before I turned to head back to my dressing room to get dressed.

"Are you a senior?" she asked.

"Yes," I said, turning back around.

"So am I."

"That sucks having to change schools your senior year."

She shrugged. "My mom got a new job, so we didn't have much choice. Do you mind giving me your phone number? Maybe you, Aidan and I can hang out before school starts."

I looked at her suspiciously. "Why do you keep trying

to hook me up with your brother? I told you I'm not interested."

She looked at the floor, embarrassed. "I'm sorry," she said. "It's just that we saw you in the mall earlier when you were sitting in the food court. Aidan mentioned how cute you were—"

"He did?" I interrupted.

"Yeah. His last girlfriend really broke his heart, and I was hoping I could find someone really nice for him. At least let me introduce you."

I didn't want to admit how much I wanted to meet Aidan. "Let me think about it while I'm changing clothes," I said.

"Okay."

I had already made up my mind before I had my clothes back on that I was going to at least meet Aidan. Since we were going to the same school, it couldn't hurt to at least introduce myself. Who was I fooling though, I wondered as I slipped my jeans back on. From a distance, Aidan Calhoun was fine, and I couldn't wait to meet him.

Nadia was waiting for me when I walked out of the dressing room.

"So what did you decide?" she asked.

"I'll meet him," I said.

She started bouncing around. "He's going to be speechless when he sees you," she said, grabbing my arm and dragging me behind her.

We walked out of the dressing room, and Aidan was standing patiently near the front door of the store.

"Aidan," Nadia said.

He turned to look in our direction, and I saw his eyes widen, but he tried to play it off.

"What's up?" he said. I assumed his words were for his sister, but his eyes were on me.

"This is Courtland. She's a senior at Grover. We'll be going to school together," she said.

He stuck out his hand. "Nice to meet you, Courtland," he said in this nice baritone voice.

I tried not to think about how much our meeting reminded me of the first time I'd really talked to Allen when we'd ended up in English class together last year.

"Nice to meet you, too," I said, shaking his hand, which was soft and warm. I looked away, not wanting him to see how much a handshake was affecting me. "Your sister said you guys moved here from Atlanta. I don't know what I'd do if my parents made me move my senior year."

"It's not that big a deal for me," Nadia said, "but Aidan is worried because he doesn't know what he's going to do about basketball. He was expected to be the top recruit this year in Atlanta, and he really wants a full scholarship to the University of Alabama."

He cut her a look like he was telling her to chill, and I wondered if I was experiencing déjà vu. This guy was starting to have too many similarities to Allen.

"Well, good luck with school," I said, realizing I

needed to get out of the store. I knew I probably sounded rude, but I didn't care. There was no way I was about to walk back down the road I had just traveled.

He looked stunned at my tone, and Nadia looked kind of confused. It wasn't until I was halfway out the entrance and the security alarm started blaring that I realized I still had the outfit I had tried on in my hands. Suddenly feeling like I was about to cry, I thrust the outfit into Nadia's hands and took off toward the table where Momma and Cory were still sitting.

"Wait," I heard Nadia yell. "You didn't give me your phone number."

I didn't even have the energy to respond. I couldn't believe God was messing with my head the way He was. Here I was trying with everything in me to get over Allen and move on with my life, and he sent a guy who was just like Allen. I didn't even want to think about falling for Aidan only to have my heart broken again. There was only so much hurt one girl could take.

three

I woke up early the next morning, dreading going to church. Ever since things had happened with Allen, I really wasn't feeling church as much, although not going wasn't an option since Momma wasn't hearing that. I tried to be a decent person and to treat people right, and I still couldn't believe God had allowed me to get into such a horrible relationship with Allen.

"Courtland, Momma said to get up," Cory came into my room and said.

"I'm up," I muttered.

Cory was already dressed, and it looked like Momma had just finished combing her hair. "You look nice," I said.

"You don't," she said, frowning.

I knew I had to look really rough for her to say that, so I hopped out of bed and went to check myself out in the mirror. I couldn't help but laugh because I did look crazy. My hair was all over my head because I hadn't bothered to wrap it the night before, and my eyes and mouth were all crusty.

My body was sore, and I realized I was awake so early because I had had the craziest dream. I tried to remember the details, but I couldn't.

"Momma said breakfast will be ready in a few minutes," Cory said.

I nodded and headed to the shower, still trying to recall the dream. Finally, I gave up, focusing instead on what I would wear to church. I thought about the first time Allen had shown up there, and I felt tears fill my eyes. I couldn't believe how he had everybody I knew fooled—my parents, Cory, members of my church. How had we all been so wrong?

I was still in a funky mood by the time I made it downstairs to breakfast. I picked at my cheese grits and only took a few bites of my sausage. Momma and Daddy must have sensed what was going on, because they let me be, and I was glad.

When we finally made it to church, I took a seat in the pews, praying Momma wouldn't force me to sing. She just looked at me and gave a smile of understanding and she squeezed my hand before she headed to the choir, her way of letting me know everything was going to be okay.

I was on the verge of dozing off when it came time for our morning prayer. Normally I couldn't wait for it to be over because the deacons always prayed these long, drawn-out prayers, but today the prayer was being led by Andrea, our Worth the Wait adviser. There was something in her voice that moved me as she prayed for the youth of our church and the world and especially for the members of Worth the Wait and our upcoming purity conference. By the time she was done, I couldn't stop the tears that were falling from my eyes.

I tried to slip out of church to go into the back fellowship hall to get myself together, but before I could, our pastor asked for all the youth to come up front and the members of our church prayed over us. When our pastor called my name, I wasn't even embarrassed, and I welcomed the prayer for my protection and I prayed that all that had happened with Allen wouldn't make me angry or bitter.

I had never experienced anything like the power I felt in our church that day. I guess I wasn't the only one in a place where I was questioning God, because all around me old people and young ones were rejoicing and asking God to touch them.

I left church determined that no matter what, I was never going to let anything or anyone get in the middle of me and my relationship with God. If I didn't love Him, there was no way I could love myself.

Before I knew it, it was two days before Momma and Daddy's wedding. School was supposed to begin the next week, and I was looking forward to it starting and the wedding being over. Momma was about to drive me crazy with all her plans.

As much as I tried not to think about Aidan, every now and then he would creep into my thoughts, but I would just shove them back, just like I did when Allen popped into my head, which was becoming less and less often, thank goodness.

I figured asking about when was too soon to start dating another guy would be a good question for starting off our first Worth the Wait meeting of the school year, so I jotted it down to remind myself to discuss it with Andrea, who was meeting with the new officers that afternoon. I was looking forward to being president of our chapter. Jennifer Perez, another member of our group, had been named vice president, and we had talked a couple of times during the summer to brainstorm ideas. My best friend, Sabrina—Bree—had been elected secretary, and I was happy I had some girls who had my back in office with me. I believed we were going to accomplish some really good things this year. The purity conference we were planning was going to be the first one in the city, and the ball that would end the weekend was going to be crazy.

"Courtland, you ready to go?" Momma yelled.

She was getting on my last nerve. "Only two more days to go," I said to my reflection in the mirror as I combed my hair. We were going to pick up our dresses for the rehearsal dinner, which was being held the next night.

"Yes," I said.

"Hurry up. We don't want to be late."

"How can you be late going to the mall?" I muttered.

When I got downstairs, Daddy was sitting in the living room watching TV, and Cory was playing her Game Boy, as usual.

"Don't forget I have a Worth the Wait meeting this afternoon," I said to Momma, hoping she would get the hint that I didn't want to spend all day on wedding plans.

"I know," she said. "We only have a few places to go." She pulled out this long list that looked like it would take five days to complete.

"Momma," I said. I looked to Daddy for help, but he just shrugged.

"What?" Momma said, but I just tuned her out, my gaze locked on the television screen. Flashing before me was a picture of Aidan Calhoun at the gym of what looked like Grover High School. "Do you hear me talking to you?"

"Shh," I said, realizing a second too late that I was talking to Momma and not one of my friends.

"Corwin, do you hear this child?" Momma complained in a tone that let me know I had lost my mind.

"Sorry," I said just to get her to be quiet. I moved closer to the television, drawn to Aidan like a magnet.

The reporter was asking him about his goals for the future since he was considered a top NBA draft pick. Aidan shrugged. "I enjoy basketball, but that's not my main focus. I won't even consider going into the NBA until after I graduate from college. My parents have always raised me to believe education is important. If it's meant for me to play ball, that will be here after I graduate."

I had to admit I was really impressed with his response. Allen had been all about getting money as soon as he could, which was why he was in so much trouble now for taking money.

The reporter asked Aidan something about all the girls who chased after him in Atlanta, and again Aidan shrugged. "I'm not going to lie and say I don't enjoy the attention," he said, and my heart sank. I was just about to walk away from the television when his next words stopped me.

"It's nice and everything, but I only have time for one girl at a time in my life, and whoever she is, she has to understand that I plan on remaining a virgin until I get married."

I thought about Aidan's words all morning, and they were still on my mind by the time I made it to the Worth the Wait officers' meeting. A couple of the officers were already there, so I smiled and waved before heading over to Andrea, who was on the phone. She looked at me and grinned, and held up a finger, letting me know she would be finished in a minute. Once she was done, she hugged me, and as always I remembered the lesson she had taught our Worth the Wait group last year.

During one of our meetings, as we walked through the door, Andrea hugged us like she always did, but once we were settled, she passed out gift boxes, which wasn't all that unusual, either. Inside each box was a slip of paper that read we had been given the gift of HIV. As we all looked around in confusion, Andrea had explained that she had contracted the virus that causes AIDS during her freshman year of college after having sex with her boyfriend once. It had taught me a huge lesson about valuing my virginity.

"How was your summer?" she asked.

I told her about the basketball camp and helping to plan my parents' wedding.

"I got my invitation. I'll be there tomorrow." I nodded. "I might need your help planning my wedding," she said and flashed an engagement ring.

I gave a little scream and started jumping around. I knew Andrea was dating a preacher named Justin Clarke, but didn't realize it was that serious. "He proposed over the summer, during church." Suddenly she looked a little sad.

"What's wrong?" I asked. "Aren't you excited?"

"Oh, yeah," she said. "I feel like bouncing off the walls. I'll go ahead and tell you and mention it to the rest of the girls during the meeting. Justin has been offered a job in Atlanta, and I'm going with him."

"Are you serious?" I said. "You're leaving us?"

Andrea was the coolest adviser I had ever met. She was only twenty-nine, but she gave really good advice, and she was a good listener, unlike my aunt Dani, who gave crazy advice and always had an opinion about everything.

I groaned thinking about Aunt Dani, realizing she was probably coming into town the next morning for my parents' wedding. I really hadn't talked to her since she had moved to Atlanta, and for the moment, I didn't have a desire to, but my granddaddy had told me he'd invited her to Momma's and Daddy's wedding, and I had a feeling she was coming. I still couldn't believe she had been seeing Allen behind my back.

"You ready to get the meeting started?" Andrea asked.

I nodded and took a seat near the front of the room. I half listened as Andrea told the other girls about moving to Atlanta. A few of them looked like they were about to cry, and part of me felt like it, too. Andrea assured us that she would help us find a new adviser and that she would be back for the purity conference, but I knew it wouldn't be the same without her.

"Courtland has an excellent question to start our first meeting." She turned to me, indicating I could have the floor.

"How soon after you break up with someone can you date someone else?" I asked.

"Immediately," a new girl named Felicity Williams said. She had only recently joined the club, and although she seemed nice on the surface, there was something about her I didn't trust. She seemed like a black version of Emily, only joining the club because she thought guys found virgins sexy. "I always date more than one guy at a time so if one breaks up with me, I have another one waiting." She seemed proud of herself, but I thought that was nasty.

"I say at least six months. Give yourself time to heal," Jennifer said.

"What if you meet someone before then?" I asked, ignoring thoughts of Aidan.

"Have you met someone?" some girl whose name I couldn't remember asked.

"No," I said defensively, wondering why she was in my business.

"She can't buy a man right now after making up all those lies about Allen Benson," Felicity said and laughed. "Talking about he tried to rape her."

I could not believe she put me on blast like that. True, most of the girls in the room probably already knew, but still.

"Felicity, remember our rules about respecting others," Andrea said. "Anyone else want to offer suggestions on how soon you should date?"

"I say let your heart decide," someone said.

That was the best advice I had heard that day.

We talked for a few more minutes then moved on to purity conference plans. My best friend, Bree, came in twenty minutes later looking like she had just rolled out of bed.

"Sorry I'm late," she said breathlessly and plopped down in a chair.

Jennifer, who had been taking notes since Bree wasn't there, passed her the notebook and pen. "How are you going to be the secretary and not be here to take notes?" she asked.

"I said I was sorry," Bree snapped. I looked at her in surprise. She was the most mild-mannered person I knew, and in the three years we had been best friends, I had never seen her really annoyed with anyone—well, anyone except me, which I deserved since I had punched her because I thought she told the whole school about Allen trying to rape me after I made her promise not to tell.

U OK? I wrote on my notebook and turned it so she could see.

She read it and nodded. I was waiting for her to write something back, but she didn't, focusing instead on taking notes.

When the meeting was finally over, I turned to her.

"What's up?" I asked.

"What are you talking about?" she said, sounding defensive.

"Are you okay?" I asked.

"Yeah. Why do you want to know?"

"You're just acting strange."

"I just have some stuff going on," she said.

"You want to talk?"

"Not really," she said.

I shrugged and changed the subject, knowing she would come talk to me when she was ready.

"So how was your summer?" I asked. It was weird asking my best friend that. For the last couple of years, we always hung out over the summer, but this year we had both been busy. Bree had participated in the Minority Journalism Workshop at the University of Alabama at Tuscaloosa and another one at Columbia in New York after volunteering at Camp Celebration at Forty-fifth Street Baptist Church.

"It was good. I'm glad that summer camp is over. Those kids were okay, but I will never be a camp counselor again."

I laughed. "I'm glad my parents didn't make me get a job."

She just nodded.

"So what's up with you and Nathaniel?" I asked. Nathaniel Dixon and I had known each other since kindergarten, and he and Bree had started dating last year.

"Nothing much. He's outside waiting for me now."

"For real?" I said, gathering my things. "Let me go say hello. I haven't seen him all summer."

She grabbed her purse, and we headed outside to where Nathaniel was parked in his old clunker, chilling and bopping his head to the beat of some song on the radio.

"Hey," I said as soon as we got close enough for him to hear us over the music.

He looked up and grinned, then got out of the car. "Hey," he said, giving me a hug. He had gotten taller, and it looked as though he had been working out, because he was sporting muscles that looked as hard as rocks.

"Look at you, trying to work out," I said, tapping one of the muscles.

He grinned, then leaned down to give Bree a kiss. "You ready?" he asked.

She nodded and got into the car.

"Hey, you guys are coming to the rehearsal dinner tonight, right?"

They looked at each other, and without saying a word, it was like they held a whole conversation.

"Come on, you guys. I need my friends there," I said when it looked like they were going to say no.

They finally agreed, which made me feel better. I said goodbye, hopped in my car and headed home. When I got there, Momma was surrounded by gifts.

"What's all this?" I asked, wondering who had sent her five of the same thing.

"I realized I hadn't picked up the gifts for the wedding party," she said, "so I had to run to the mall." She glanced at the clock. "I have so much to do. The rehearsal starts in two hours, and I still have to wrap these gifts, get dressed and get over to the church."

"I'll take care of the gifts," I said, taking a pair of scissors and some tape from her.

She looked relieved. "Thank you, Courtland," she said.

"Where are Dad and Cory?" I asked as I got settled in front of the pile of presents.

"They had to run to the store to get some stuff for the rehearsal dinner."

"I'm surprised you let them," I said, and she swatted her hand at me.

"Have I been that bad?" she asked.

"Pretty much," I said before I could stop myself. "You just seem a little obsessed." I hoped this didn't sound as bad. The truth was Momma had gotten crazy.

"I'm sorry," she said. "I just want this day to be perfect. This is something I've dreamed of for years, and I had given up hope it was going to happen."

"It's okay, Momma. Tomorrow is going to be great."

"You think so?" she asked, looking worried.

"I know so," I said.

The next morning, I heard Momma up around four o'clock. I knew she was nervous because the wedding rehearsal had been disastrous. Her best friend's flight had been delayed, so she had missed the rehearsal entirely, and several members of the wedding party had gotten lost, so they were late getting there. Practice started an hour late, and even then no one could seem to get it together. People were laughing and joking instead of listening to the coordinator, a lady named Mrs. Henley whom everyone called Mrs. Bertie. I had to admit the name fit, because she looked just like Big Bird. She had on this yellow outfit and blue eyeshadow, and she had teased the front of her hair like some of the actresses used to do in those old movies I saw from the eighties.

Momma had finally gotten so angry, she went clean off, then she started crying. Daddy finally took her into the back of the church and talked to her for a little while, and she seemed fine—until we got to the rehearsal dinner, which was being held at the Hoover Lake House. The caterer spilled two trays of food on his way inside, so there wasn't enough for everyone. The kids ended up eating McDonald's, which was fine with me, but Momma was not happy.

I snuck out of bed and found Momma downstairs in the living room just sitting on the sofa.

"Momma," I whispered into the darkness. "You okay?"

"Yes," she whispered back.

I took a seat next to her. "Are you nervous?"

"A little," she admitted. "What was I thinking, trying to plan a wedding in a few months at my age?"

Momma was only thirty-nine, so it wasn't like she was really old. "It was your first step toward learning to love yourself," I reminded her and she smiled.

"That's right," she murmured. "That was the best advice you ever gave me, to demand your daddy marry me, but maybe it wasn't the right thing to do. Maybe I shouldn't have insisted, you know? Maybe this isn't what he wants."

"Momma, y'all have been together forever. Why are you suddenly feeling bad for wanting to get married? You've been telling me all my life to wait until I found someone who really loves me to get married and have kids."

"You're right," she said. "Thank you, Courtland. I needed to hear that."

"Are you going back to bed?" I asked.

She shook her head. "I can't sleep," she said. "I'm so used to your daddy sleeping next to me. It feels weird not having him there."

"You're the one who didn't want him to see you until the wedding," I reminded her. Daddy was spending the night at his Alcoholics Anonymous sponsor's house.

"I know," she said.

"I'll sleep with you," I offered.

I felt her smile in the darkness. "Thank you. You're a good daughter, Courtland."

"You're a good mother," I said, leaning over to give her a hug.

"So how are you doing?" she asked. "I can't remember the last time we talked. How are you dealing with this whole Allen thing?"

"I'm okay," I said. "I wonder if I shouldn't have dropped the charges. People think I made up what happened."

"People are always going to have something to say," she said. "You had to do what's right for you. You know your daddy and I support you whatever you decide to do. You wanted to move on with your life, so we have to respect that."

"Thank you," I said. "I just don't know how to explain my decision to Cory. She's asked me a couple of times why we're not going to court and why Allen's not going to jail. I don't really know what to say to her. She feels like she did something wrong because she videotaped what happened then kept Aunt Dani's cell phone for a while without saying anything."

"I'll talk to her," Momma promised. She patted my knee. "Come on. Let's try and get a few more hours of sleep."

I followed her upstairs to her room, and we jumped into bed. It reminded me of the times when I was a little girl, before Cory was born, when we would snuggle together in her bed on the nights Daddy was working.

"This is going to be a good year for us," Momma said into the darkness.

"I hope so," I said.

When I woke up a few hours later, there was a foot in my face. I moved it out of the way and looked down to find Cory in the bed. I figured she had come into Momma's room at some point after we had fallen asleep, and as usual, she was sleeping wild. Momma's side of the bed was empty, so I went searching for her. I heard voices in the kitchen and smelled bacon.

I was about to fuss at Momma for cooking on her wedding day, but I stopped short when I saw her best friend, Brenda Caldwell, sitting at the table. They each had a steaming cup of coffee in front of them and were laughing about something.

"Good morning," I said, really more for Momma. I still wasn't speaking to her friend, who had annoyed me so much when she was Grover's cheerleading adviser that I still refused to use her name.

"Good morning," they both said.

Momma's friend got up to hug me, but I couldn't

make myself hug her back. She didn't seem to notice the awkwardness. She let me go and walked over to the stove where she flipped the bacon and checked on what looked like homemade biscuits in the oven.

"How've you been, Courtland?" she asked, looking over her shoulder.

"Fine," I said. "Momma, do you need me to do anything?"

"No, baby. Everything's done. I'm just waiting on the woman to come and do my makeup and hair, then we'll be ready."

I nodded. "I'll go wake Cory," I said and left the room before anyone could say anything.

Cory was just waking up when I finally walked into the room after making a pit stop at the bathroom. "Morning, munchkin," I said.

She squinted at me, then went into her room for her glasses. Once she returned with them on, she smiled.

"Morning," she said and yawned.

"Breakfast is almost ready.

"Okay."

"You ready for the day?"

For a second, Cory looked excited until she spotted the dress she was supposed to wear. "Do I have to wear that?" she complained.

"Come on, munchkin. The dress looks really nice on you."

She didn't look convinced. "I'll wear the dress if you remember to stop calling me munchkin. I'm too old for you to call me that. I don't like it, just like you don't like to be called Corky anymore."

She had a point. I couldn't stand that nickname. It reminded me of when I was fat.

"Deal," I said. "Please don't give Momma a hard time today, okay? Let her enjoy the day. I know you don't want to wear the dress, but do it for Momma and Daddy."

Mentioning Daddy reminded me that maybe he wasn't up yet, so I decided to call him. I tried his cell phone, but it went straight to voice mail. When I remembered he had given me the number at his sponsor's house just in case I needed to get in touch with him, I hurried to my room to get my cell phone where I had stored the number.

The phone only rang twice before someone answered.

"Good morning," someone said. I couldn't tell whether it was a man or a woman.

"Good morning," I said. "This is Courtland. Is my dad there?"

The person on the other end hesitated then told me to hold on. I heard someone whispering in the background, but I couldn't make out what they were saying. Finally, the person came back to the line. "He can't come to the phone right now. Can I have him call you back?"

The person's answer kind of surprised me. Last year someone had broken into our house, and Daddy had shot him to death. It wasn't until months later that we found out Aunt Dani was behind the whole break-in.

She was so deep in debt she had convinced one of her boyfriends to steal from her own family. Since then, Daddy had changed a lot. I couldn't remember the last time he hadn't taken a call from me.

"I was just calling to make sure he was up," I said. "Just tell him if he needs me to give me a call. Otherwise, I'll see him at church."

"Okay," the person said and hung up.

The call was weird, but I didn't have much time to think about it before Momma was yelling for us to come eat. I didn't say much during breakfast, not really wanting to talk to Momma's friend, but it wasn't like she noticed since she and Momma talked nonstop.

As I was clearing the table, the doorbell rang.

"That must be the hairstylist," Momma said.

"I'll get it," I said. I hurried to the door and received a shock when I saw Aunt Dani standing there—at least I thought it was Aunt Dani. She had lost a lot of weight, and her hair was cut really short. She had on a tight red shirt that showed off her big breast implants and her stomach, including her pooch, and some shorts that my mother would never have allowed me to wear. Seriously, I didn't know how she could move they were so tight. Her red heels were about six inches high, and I wondered how she managed to walk in them.

"Hey, Corky," she said, walking into the house without even waiting to be invited in. She brushed a kiss on my cheek, and I tried not to recoil. I hadn't seen her since she'd left the hospital after Allen ran over her. I had thought about calling her a few times to check on her, but then I realized she needed to be the one calling me so she could apologize for seeing my boyfriend behind my back.

I was just closing the door when I felt a weight against it on the other side. I pulled it open to see what was going on, and her boyfriend, Miles, was standing there weighed down with suitcases.

"Hey, Miles," I said, grabbing a small one that slipped from under his arm.

"Hey, Courtland. Thanks for getting that for me. How have you been?"

"Good," I said. "Why are you bringing all those suitcases in? Aren't you guys staying at a hotel or something?"

"We are, but we won't be able to check in until after noon. Your aunt couldn't decide what to wear, so she wanted to look at everything she had brought again."

I nodded, wondering where Aunt Dani was planning on storing all those bags—there were about five of them—and changing.

My question was answered when she came out of the kitchen with a biscuit in her hand and instructed Miles to put the bags in my room. I tried not to let my annoyance show. Aunt Dani hadn't even been there five minutes, and she was already getting on my nerves.

Momma looked annoyed, too, when she came out of the kitchen.

"Dani, I really wish you had told me you were coming over here," she was saying. "Why didn't you go to Daddy's?"

"Why? We're sisters. I don't need an invitation to come to your house—unless something has changed." Momma and Aunt Dani were really half-sisters, but for as long as I could remember Aunt Dani had always been at family events.

I could tell Momma wanted to say something, and so did I, but I knew it wasn't the time. I was determined Momma was going to have a good day.

"Miles, I'll help you with those bags," I said.

"Thank you," he said. I grabbed a medium-size case and took that along with the smaller one up to my room while Aunt Dani just stood there like I was her servant. When we finally made it to my room, I flung the cases onto my unmade bed while Miles neatly lined his up on the floor next to my desk.

"Why are you with her?" I found myself asking.

For a second I wondered if Miles was going to answer. "I love her," he finally said.

"But she cheated on you, and she lied about being pregnant by the other guy," I said.

Miles shrugged. "You've never lied about something?" he asked.

"Well, yeah," I said, "but never anything that serious."

"She said she was sorry," he said.

"And you believe her? She wouldn't even be with you if Allen had told her he wanted to be with her. She's just gonna leave you for the next guy who comes along."

"I doubt that," he said, but I could see some doubt in his eyes.

"You don't think she's going to do this again?" I asked. "Aunt Dani hasn't changed. She's still chasing money."

"She has changed," he insisted.

"What makes you think that?" I asked.

"Because we're married now."

My mouth dropped open. "What?" I shrieked so loud Momma called upstairs, "Courtland, you okay?"

I was too shocked to speak, so Miles yelled back, "She's fine."

A few seconds later, we heard footsteps, then Aunt Dani walked into the room. "I just wanted to make sure you weren't trying to steal my man," she said, walking over to Miles and wrapping her arms around him, clinging to him. She stood on her tiptoes and kissed him on the lips, and while her back was to me, I caught sight of the tattoo she must have recently gotten in the small of her back. I only had a chance to glance at it, but it looked like the butterfly Mariah Carey got right after she married Nick Cannon. I wondered briefly if she had Miles's name somewhere in it the way Mariah had *Mrs. Cannon* as the body of her butterfly.

Seeing the tattoo made me sick to my stomach, but I ignored it and focused on what she'd said. Her words made me lose it. "You mean the way you stole mine?" I asked. "Please. Miles and I were just talking—actually, about you. Unlike you, I have class and would never steal someone else's man, especially someone who is related to me."

Aunt Dani looked at me. "Girl, are you still mad about me hooking up with Allen?" She said it in front of Miles like it was no big deal.

Before I could stop myself, I lunged for her, but Miles grabbed me before I could get there.

"Donna, you need to come get your daughter," Aunt Dani yelled, but I could tell she was scared because her voice shook. "She's acting like she's lost her mind."

I struggled to get free from Miles, determined I was going to beat my aunt like she had stolen something. I had never been the fighting type, but Aunt Dani had pushed me too far. "Allen was my boyfriend, and you were seeing him. Not to mention you and some other guy broke into our house and stole from us. I can't believe you had the nerve to show your face here again."

By that time, Momma was upstairs. She took in the scene, and I thought she was going to have something to say to me for the way I was talking to Aunt Dani, but instead she turned to her. "Dani, I think you need to leave. We have a lot to do today, and I wasn't expecting you. Now isn't a good time."

Momma's words seemed to hurt Aunt Dani more than the lick I was about to give her ever could. "You don't want me in your house, Donna?"

Momma didn't say a word.

"Y'all are mad because I took a few things from your house and I hooked up with a guy who wasn't even interested in Corky? Y'all can't be serious." She looked at Miles. "Come on. We're not staying where we're not welcome." She stomped out of the room, cursing up a storm every step of the way. I had never heard her use profanity, but I realized even though I had known Aunt Dani all my life, I didn't know her at all.

Miles gathered up the bags and then hesitated. "I'm sorry for what Loretta did," he said, calling her by her first name, which no one in our family ever did. "She really has changed, and she feels really bad for stealing from you and for what Allen did to Courtland. She was the one who talked me into turning him in to the NBA officials for the money he had been taking."

I thought Miles was cool, but his words really weren't impressing me.

When he realized neither Momma nor I was going to say anything, he apologized again then clumsily walked down the stairs. I heard him speak to Cory, then he and Aunt Dani were gone, and I realized I would be fine if I never saw her again. No matter what Miles believed, I knew Aunt Dani wasn't sorry for what she had done. She was just sorry she had gotten caught.

"I'm sorry for messing up your day, Momma," I said, walking over to give her a hug.

"You didn't," she said. "I guess your granddaddy must have told Dani about the wedding since I didn't invite her, and for her to think she could come over to our house after all that's happened and not even apologize..." She just shook her head.

"Donna, the stylist is here," her friend called.

"Let's pretend that never happened," Momma suggested.

That was just fine by me.

four

AS the sounds of the song "Because You Loved Me" filled the church, Momma walked toward Daddy looking like a real live princess. By the time she finally made it to his side, they were both in tears and so was I. In a lot of ways, the wedding was like a new beginning for our family.

It was as if I was outside myself watching them give their vows. They both looked so happy, and I prayed it would always be this way, and that one day I would find that type of happiness. Aidan Calhoun's face popped into my head, and I wondered if he had thought of me since that day we'd met at the mall. I couldn't wait to see him at school to apologize for the way I had acted. I had done some research on him on the Internet, and he really did seem like a nice guy.

I had even found a picture of him and had printed it out and had put it in my journal.

Momma and Daddy finally said their "I Do's," and

when they kissed, although part of me wanted to throw up in my mouth because they were too old for all that, another part of me thought it was kind of sweet. They grabbed hands and they were just about to head down the aisle when Daddy stopped and came to take my hand and Momma took Cory's and we all walked out as the audience applauded.

"I's married now," Momma said, twirling the skirt of her dress. I couldn't help but laugh. We had watched *The Color Purple* a few months ago and one of the characters had said the same thing.

We all laughed and stood around talking about how well everything had gone until Mrs. Bertie, the wedding coordinator, stomped into the church foyer and insisted we come back in for pictures. We took so many pictures, I thought my face was gonna freeze from smiling so much. When the photographer called for members of Daddy's family to gather for a group shot, I felt really bad for him. He had been adopted when he was a baby, and both his parents had since passed away. They were both only children, too, so there wasn't anyone to stand with him other than me and Cory. A few of his friends from the police department jumped in a few of the photos, clowning for the camera, as did some of the members of Alcoholics Anonymous.

I saw the photographer hesitate before calling for Momma's side of the family to gather for photos. He looked relieved when about twenty people jumped up. Of course, my grandparents were there along with

Momma's aunts, uncles and cousins. We all gathered together, squeezing in tight. The photographer was just about to snap the picture when a loud voice called out, "Wait for me."

I looked up, not believing what I was seeing. Truthfully, after we'd put Aunt Dani out of the house, I thought she and Miles had returned to Atlanta since I didn't see them at the wedding, but obviously I was wrong. Aunt Dani came strolling down the middle aisle of the church, looking like it was *her* wedding day. She had on a white dress that was entirely too tight with a short train. She snatched the bouquet from Momma's best friend, then had the nerve to carve out a spot right next to Momma, who was so angry I thought we were about to witness a WWE championship wrestling match.

"Dani," my granddaddy said in a warning tone.

"Hey, Daddy," she said, sounding all innocent. "We'll talk after the pictures." She moved in closer to Momma who had no choice but to take a step back, putting Aunt Dani right in the middle of the picture. "Come on," she said to the photographer. "We don't have all day. We're about to go get our party on."

The photographer stood there, looking at Momma in confusion, trying to figure out what to do.

I felt someone push past me and looked up to see Granddaddy yanking Aunt Dani out of the picture and marching her out of the church past Miles, who was looking like a tourist in New York City with a big camera hanging around his neck. He looked at Momma apologetically and rushed after Aunt Dani and Grand-daddy.

Momma looked like she wanted to cry, and Daddy pulled her to him, kissing her on the forehead and whispering something in her ear. For the second time that day, Aunt Dani had tried to ruin Momma's perfect day, but like Daddy, I was determined that wasn't going to happen.

"Come on, everybody," I said, ignoring Mrs. Bertie as I stepped out of line so I could get everyone assembled again. Under my direction, people shifted around so they were once again surrounding Momma, and once everyone was in place, I jumped back in the picture, ignoring the pain in my cheeks as I smiled as hard as I could.

When we were finally done, Mrs. Bertie announced the limos had arrived, and we all piled in for the ride to the Harbert Center. Momma and Daddy had a car to themselves, and since there were only a handful of people in our car, I told Bree she could ride with me. Mrs. Bertie had a fit, insisting that only members of the wedding party could ride in the limo. Bree just shrugged and jumped into Nathaniel's car. They both looked so happy as they drove away with Bree yelling she'd see me at the reception.

I expected the party to be in full swing by the time we made it to the reception since we had spent more than an hour taking pictures, but to my surprise, people were just kind of sitting around waiting for us to get there. After all the members of the wedding party were announced, dinner was served. I had gone with Momma the day she'd had the tasting, and I thought the chicken breast on top of a pile of wild rice and spinach was good then, but it was amazing at the reception—or maybe I was just hungry.

After the meal, a few members of the wedding party gave toasts, then Momma and Daddy had to throw the bouquet and garter. When my Worth the Wait adviser, Andrea, caught Momma's bouquet, I couldn't help but laugh since the way it looked, she really would be the next one to get married. Things got even funnier when her fiancé, Justin, whom I met for the first time that night, caught the garter. All the guys were riding him, but it didn't seem to bother him. He couldn't take his eyes off Andrea as they danced together in honor of catching the garter and bouquet, just like Daddy couldn't take his eyes off Momma during their first dance, and I found myself wondering if a guy would ever look at me like that and want to spend the rest of his life with me. Allen had told me that he wanted to be with me, but I realized he was just saying what he thought I wanted to hear. I wanted to find a guy who really meant it.

When Aidan Calhoun's face popped into my mind, I couldn't help but smile. As much as I wanted to pretend I didn't want to get into another relationship so soon after what had happened with Allen, the thought of being with Aidan had me really rethinking all that. Suddenly, I couldn't wait for school.

* * *

I was up long before the alarm went off the first day of senior year, excited about seeing Aidan again. Momma and Daddy had only taken a mini-honeymoon because she didn't want to miss our first day of school. She and Daddy had come home from Destin, Florida, the night before looking relaxed and so happy.

"Good morning, Miss Senior," Momma greeted me when I made it to the breakfast table.

"Good morning," I said, giving her a kiss on the cheek. "Hey, Cory," I said to my sister, who as usual was engrossed in her Game Boy. "Hey, Daddy," I said, a little surprised to see him there. He was starting to eat with us more, but he normally was already at work by the time we had breakfast. "You don't have to work today?"

He looked at Momma and smiled. "We decided to take the day off to enjoy our honeymoon a little longer while you kids are at school. Right, baby?" He got up and kissed Momma on the neck, and she blushed and giggled like she was in high school.

I got an image of my parents together and felt sick to my stomach. "That's enough," I said. "We're still your kids and some stuff we don't ever need to know."

Daddy ignored me and continued nuzzling Momma's neck. Cory and I looked at each other and she seemed as disgusted as I was starting to feel.

"Seriously, could you guys stop?" I complained.

Finally, Daddy sat down and Momma went back to

the stove where she placed waffles and bacon on plates for each of us, served us then sat down and grabbed Cory's Game Boy, ignoring her protest. Daddy grabbed my hand and Momma's, which was my signal to take Cory's, who then took Momma's. We bowed our heads as Momma said grace, thanking God for the food as well as for a wonderful wedding and asking Him to bless us during the school year.

"So do you want me to drop Cory off at school?" I asked. I had been meaning to ask her but we had been so busy with wedding plans it had slipped my mind. I was looking forward to being able to drive myself to school. Momma and Daddy had gotten me a Toyota Tercel for my birthday in December, but they hadn't really let me start driving it until over the summer. Part of me wondered if they were going to let me drive to school. I had already made up my mind if they had something to say we were just going to have a conversation. I was the only girl I knew who had a car and still couldn't drive half the time, and it was starting to get old.

"Oh, Courtland, would you?" she asked, looking grateful.

I nodded since I had a mouthful of waffles.

Once we were done, Cory and I kissed Momma and Daddy and headed off.

"So, you excited about the first day of school?" I asked after we had been driving for a few minutes. Cory was going into the fourth grade, and I remembered how nervous she had been last year.

"Yes," she said, looking really excited. "Destini's going to be in my class again this year."

She and Destini had met last year and become good friends. Destini had come over to our house a few times, and she was a really sweet little girl. I wanted to ask her what it was like being in foster care, but I didn't want to make her sad, so I didn't.

"That should be fun," I said.

"Are you excited?" Cory asked me, her eyes big behind her glasses, which took up half her face.

"Yeah," I said. "I'm finally a senior. This time next year, I'll be going off to college."

I already had a few schools in mind, and I realized I needed to narrow my choices down soon since I needed to start applying.

"You're not going to stay here for college?" Cory asked.

We had talked about me leaving a couple of times, and obviously she didn't like the thought of it since she was pretending to forget all about the conversations.

"No," I said patiently.

"But why not? There are colleges here," she said.

"I know, but I want to go away to school and experience being on my own," I explained.

"You could stay on campus at one of the schools here," she pointed out.

"Yeah, I could, but I don't think it would be the same."

"I'm going to miss you," she said, looking like she was about to cry.

"I'll miss you, too, but that's not until next year, so we have a while, okay?"

She nodded and stared out the window.

"Why did you drop the charges against Allen?" she said after a few seconds. I didn't know how she had found out, and I really didn't know how to explain my decision, but I did the best I could.

"I just wanted to move on with my life," I said, relieved when I saw her school up ahead. "I don't know how else to explain it."

"Is Allen going to try and hurt me the way he did you and Aunt Dani?" she asked. Something in her voice told me she had been thinking about this for a while.

"No," I said. I pulled up in front of Epic, a school for smart kids, and put the car in gear, then turned to face her. "I don't think Allen is still in Birmingham. I heard he was supposed to be moving," I lied. Really I had heard he was going to community college, but Cory didn't need to know all that. "Besides, even if he was still around, I wouldn't let him hurt you." She didn't look too convinced, so I changed the subject. "Hurry up. You don't want to be late the first day," I said.

She grabbed her backpack and reached for the door.

"Have a good day. I love you," I said. I bent over to give my little sister a hug and a kiss. Cory really was a good kid, and I knew I would miss her a lot when I left next year for school.

"Love you, too," she said, hugging me back.

* * *

By the time I made it to Grover on Birmingham's south side, the student parking lot was almost full. I found a space at the very end of the lot and gathered my things, suddenly feeling naked without my pompoms. I had decided not to try out for the cheerleader squad again, although I was supposed to be captain. Momma and I had talked a lot last year about learning to love ourselves, and I realized that part of me doing that was learning to be honest with myself, and really I wanted to play basketball, so that's what I was planning to do.

I called Bree as I was walking up the inclined driveway to Grover, but her phone went straight to voice mail. I spoke to a few kids, ignoring the strange looks I was getting. I saw a few of them whispering, and I heard the name *Allen,* but I kept on walking like I hadn't heard anything.

When I finally made it to the auditorium, I searched the crowd for Bree, and she must have been watching for me because she waved to get my attention.

I had almost reached her when someone grabbed my shirt.

"Courtland," a girl said.

I looked back to see Nadia, the girl I had met at the mall. "Hey," I said, giving her a hug. She looked a little surprised, but eventually returned it. "It's good to see you again." I tried to look for Aidan on the sly, but she must have known what I was doing because she grinned.

"He's talking to the basketball coach," she said.

"Who?" I asked, trying to look puzzled.

"Oh, it's like that?" she said, and we both laughed.

"Come sit with us," I said, grabbing her arm before she could say anything.

Bree and Nathaniel were sitting holding hands when we walked up. "Hey," I said, plopping down next to Bree. "This is my friend Nadia. She and her brother, Aidan, just moved here from Atlanta."

They exchanged greetings as Nadia sat down and Bree threw me a look, silently asking if I was referring to the Aidan I had told her about. I nodded.

Nadia placed her bag in the empty seat next to her. "Aidan should be here soon," she said, and I felt cartwheels start up in my stomach. I wondered if he would even remember me.

"I'm sorry about the way I acted when we met," I said just as Principal Abernathy stood to speak. "I just had a bunch of stuff going on."

"It's cool. I told Aidan that you were really nice, so he understood."

I smiled, relieved.

"He's been talking about you a lot since then," she said.

It felt like my heart and the cartwheels going on in my stomach were playing volleyball. "For real?" I said.

She nodded. "I tried to find your number, but you're not listed in the phone book."

"My dad's a cop, so my parents don't list our home

address and phone number," I whispered. "Give me your phone and I'll program it."

She passed me her cell phone just as Principal Abernathy was finishing up a repeat of the same boring greeting he gave every year.

Just as I passed Nadia her phone, I caught a movement out of the corner of my eye, and when I caught sight of him, my heart stopped. I must have gotten real tense, because Bree turned around, and I heard her say, "What's he doing here?"

Slowly, a blanket of whispers covered the room as I just sat there frozen, not believing who was walking toward me. Allen Benson was strolling in late, just like he did last year, looking as though he was right on time. He still looked the same—low-cut fade, sexy biceps and dimple in his cheek—but unlike last year when I thought I would melt at the sight of him, this time, for the most part, all I felt was disgust.

I had heard rumors that Allen hadn't been at the graduation ceremony last year, but I thought it was because of all the legal trouble he was in, not because he didn't graduate.

"Mr. Benson, thank you for gracing us with your presence. Please take a seat," Principal Abernathy said.

Allen continued trading handshakes and bumping shoulders with people like he hadn't heard, and I slid down in my seat, praying he wouldn't see me. I just didn't feel like dealing with him. I'd thought I would never have to see him again, and now it turned out I would have to see him every day.

I was so busy trying not to let Allen see me that it took me a second to realize Aidan had slid in next to Nadia. He leaned forward, totally ignoring his sister. "Hey, Courtland. Good to see you again," he said.

Suddenly, all thoughts of Allen were gone. I stared into Aidan's brown eyes, and I was lost.

"I couldn't wait to see you," I said and blushed. I couldn't believe I had actually said that out loud. Aidan and Nadia grinned, and I felt Bree nudging me. "I mean..."

I didn't know what to say, so I fell silent.

"I couldn't wait to see you, either," Aidan admitted, and I smiled.

I looked at Bree and she gave a little nod, letting me know she had heard him.

I didn't hear anything else that was said during the program. Even Allen's presence on the very front row didn't bother me. Every now and then I would feel Aidan's eyes on me, and when I thought he wasn't looking, I would glance over at him. His slight smile let me know that he knew what I was doing.

After orientation, the five of us stood around comparing class schedules, and I was happy when I realized I had at least one class with each of my friends. I was just about to head to homeroom when the hairs on the back of my neck stood up. I didn't have to turn around to know Allen was somewhere nearby.

He walked up to me, ignoring everyone else that was in the group.

"Hey, baby," he said and kissed me. I was so shocked I didn't move. I saw Aidan frown out of the corner of my eye.

"What are you doing?" I finally managed to say, swiping my hand across my mouth, trying to erase the kiss that I had once craved.

"Oh, you're still mad at me?" Allen looked around. "You know we had a little misunderstanding last year, and Courtland's been mad at me all summer. Isn't it time you let it go, baby? You know I love you."

He slung his arm around my shoulder, and I stood there, not believing what was happening. I guess Bree and Nathaniel were shocked, too, because it took Bree a second to say, "Get your hands off her. I can't believe you came over here after what you did to her."

Allen looked really confused. "What did I do?" he asked.

I looked around to see who was listening, and although it seemed as though half the auditorium was focused on us, I didn't care. "You tried to rape me," I said through gritted teeth, "and you ran over my aunt with your car. Let's not also forget the fact that you bet your friends you could sleep with me."

Nadia grabbed my arm and gasped.

"You need to leave," Nathaniel said, stepping in front of me.

A look of annoyance passed over Allen's face.

"What?" he said. "Aren't you the guy who tried to hit on my girl last year?"

Nathaniel didn't even bother to respond. I hadn't seen him angry since we were little kids, but when he was, it wasn't a pretty sight. I saw a vein throbbing in his neck, and I knew things were about to get ugly.

"Allen, you need to leave me alone," I said, wondering what I had ever seen in him.

He reached for me, but Nathaniel blocked him.

"I think you need to leave," Aidan said, coming to my rescue.

"Who are you?" Allen said, then a look of recognition crossed his face. "You're that new player from Atlanta. Oh, what, you're seeing my girl now?"

Aidan turned to me. "Is he your boyfriend?" he asked. I shook my head. "No."

"Do you want him to be?" he asked.

"No," I said and looked Allen dead in the eye. "I don't want to have anything to do with him. I want him to leave me alone."

"You heard the lady," Aidan said.

Allen looked like he was going to say something to me, but instead he turned to Aidan. He got up in his face, I guess to try and intimidate him, but since he and Aidan were about the same height, it didn't work.

"You can have my leftovers. I didn't want her, anyway," he said. He looked back at me and laughed. "Just so you know, she's a lousy kisser."

I felt my eyes fill with tears, not believing he'd said

that in front of the whole school. Bree grabbed my hand and squeezed and Nadia, who was still holding my arm, pulled me close.

"What did I ever do to you?" I asked Allen.

He stepped away from Aidan and gave this dry laugh. "It's what you didn't do, Little Miss Pure," he said. "Everybody has sex before they get married now."

"Not everybody," Aidan said. I didn't know him well, but I could tell he was really angry.

"Aidan," Nadia said in warning.

He ignored her. "I think you owe Courtland an apology."

"Why should I apologize to her?" Allen asked. "She should be apologizing to me. She had me chasing after her for all those months for nothing."

"You need to apologize," Aidan repeated, his tone very low.

"I'm not apologizing for nothing. She's not even worth an apology." He spat at me, and the glob landed at my feet.

In a flash, Nathaniel had jumped on Allen, and Aidan wasn't far behind. They began beating him as us girls stood there screaming. A few of Allen's basketball friends ran over and jumped in, and in a matter of seconds there were arms and legs flying in every direction. Some of the male teachers and custodians ran over trying to break the guys up as the other students stood there chanting, "Fight, fight."

People were running from all directions, and I just

stood there with my mouth open, not believing what was happening.

The staff finally managed to separate the guys, and although it was hard to tell Nathaniel and Aidan had even been in a fight, Allen looked horrible. He had a black eye and a bloody nose, and his clothes were ripped. His friends who had jumped in were pretty messed up, too.

Allen tried to save face by coming toward Aidan like he was going to do something, but I saw the relief in his eyes when one of the custodians grabbed him and dragged him off.

"You're going to be sorry for this, Courtland," he yelled.

With everything in me, I knew it wasn't just an empty threat. I knew it was a promise.

five

I felt really bad that Nathaniel and Aidan both got suspended for protecting me. Principal Abernathy was sympathetic, but Grover had a zero-tolerance policy for fighting, so the guys, along with Allen and all his basketball buddies, got suspended for two days each.

The fight was the talk of the school, and everywhere I went I heard people whispering my name or saw them averting their eyes when I walked past them. I couldn't wait for the day to be over, but it just dragged on. The only real bright spot was the mention of basketball tryouts, which would be taking place in a couple of weeks. I knew playing over the summer had me on top of my game, and I couldn't wait to get back on the court.

Momma had called and left a message for me to pick up Cory on my way home from school, so I stopped by Epic to scoop her up, and she looked really excited.

"How was the first day?" I asked.

"It was good," she said. "Destini's in my class again, and I made some more friends."

I hadn't seen Cory so excited in a long time, and it felt really good.

"That's great," I said. "Maybe we can ask Momma if you can have a slumber party and invite all your friends over."

Cory looked doubtful. "You think they'll come?"

"Sure," I said, praying they would. "We'll ask Momma as soon as we get home. I'm sure she'll say yes, and we'll plan something really fun to do while they're there."

"Will you be home?" she asked as I jumped on I-65.

"I wouldn't want to be anywhere else," I said, realizing I meant it. "Maybe I'll even invite some of my friends."

Cory grinned again then talked nonstop all the way home about everything that had happened at school, which was really unusual for her. I didn't realize until we were home that she hadn't taken her Game Boy out of the glove compartment once to play it.

When we finally made it home, Momma and Daddy were sitting up under each other on the couch. The TV was on, but they weren't really watching it.

"Hey, girls," Daddy said. "How was school?"

I let Cory go first, and she didn't stop talking for almost ten minutes. Momma and Daddy just looked at each other and smiled.

"Can I have a snack?" Cory asked when she was done.

Momma jumped up. "I'm sorry," she said. "I've been so busy all day that I forgot to make a snack."

"What have you been doing?" Cory asked.

Momma and Daddy exchanged a look and started grinning, and I just shook my head, having a good idea how they had spent the day. They were too old for that mess, but it was their honeymoon.

"We just hung out," Daddy said. He stood and gave Momma a kiss on the neck, and she blushed.

Momma told Cory to go wash up, and I followed Momma into the kitchen, not really surprised when I didn't see any boxes or unthawing meat on the counter, which would give a clue to what she was cooking for dinner.

"I figured we'd order pizza tonight," she said after noticing my gaze.

I just nodded and grabbed some plates when she pulled out some carrots, celery and ranch dressing.

"How was school?" she asked with her back to me.

I'd known she would ask at some point, and I had debated what I was going to say. Before I could stop myself, I said, "Allen's at school. He didn't graduate."

Momma slowly turned around, cocking her head like she hadn't heard me correctly. "He didn't graduate?" she repeated slowly.

I shook my head.

"So he's going to be going to school with you every day?"

I nodded.

"Corwin," Momma yelled.

Something in her voice alerted Daddy there was a problem, and he came running.

"Tell him," Momma instructed.

I repeated what I'd said about Allen not graduating, and Daddy stood there calmly. "Did he say anything to you?" he finally asked.

I sighed, told them about Allen spitting on me and Nathaniel and Aidan fighting and getting suspended, and Daddy's eyes got darker and darker, like a storm brewing in the distance.

Momma looked like she was about to cry as she walked over to examine me. "Are you okay? Did he hurt you?" she asked, running her hands over me like she was checking for broken bones.

"I'm fine," I said, stepping back.

"You're changing schools," Daddy said, and his tone told me I shouldn't argue, but I couldn't let that happen.

"I can't change schools," I said. "It's my senior year. I'm not going to let Allen drive me away from Grover. I have a right to be there, too."

"Courtland, we really would feel better if you changed schools. I don't feel comfortable with you being around him every day. All I'm going to do is worry."

"Momma, I probably won't even see him. I think he only failed one class," I said, although I knew it had to be more than that for him to be back at Grover. "Please, don't make me change schools my last year." I felt myself welling up. Allen had already done enough damage in my life. I wasn't about to let him get away with making me go to another school my senior year. "I promise, if I have any more problems, I'll let you know, then I'll go to another school."

Momma looked doubtful, so I walked over and gave her a hug. "I'm going to be fine," I said. "Allen isn't crazy enough to say or do anything else to me. Almost everyone at school saw him."

Finally she nodded and looked me directly in my eyes. "Promise me you'll let us know if you have any problems with Allen."

"If he even looks at you the wrong way, I want to know," Daddy said from behind me.

"Okay," I said, praying it wouldn't come to that. "Can we not tell Cory?"

"Tell Cory what?" she said, walking into the kitchen with her Game Boy. She plopped down in a chair, and when no one responded, she looked up, waiting for an answer.

"Tell Cory I asked about you having a slumber party," I improvised. "I knew you wanted to ask Momma, but I was just giving her a heads-up." I threw Momma and Daddy a look, and they both seemed to be in agreement that we shouldn't say anything to Cory about Allen still being at Grover.

"Can I have a slumber party?" Cory asked, getting excited all over again at the thought.

"I think that sounds like a great idea," Momma said.

"How about this weekend? We can make some invitations tonight."

Cory grinned and nodded so hard I thought her glasses were going to fall off.

Momma gave her her snack, but suddenly I wasn't hungry, so I headed up to my room. I threw myself across my bed, reached for the phone and called Nathaniel, who I realized I hadn't talked to on the phone since he and Bree had started dating.

When Bree answered, I pulled the phone from my ear, thinking I had dialed the wrong number, but it was definitely Nathaniel's digits in the phone.

"Bree?" I said.

"Hey, girl," she said.

"What are you doing answering Nathaniel's phone?"

"I always answer his phone," she said as though it was no big deal.

"Oh," I said, not knowing how else to respond. "Can I speak to him?"

"Hold on." I heard her saying something, then Nathaniel came on the line.

"What's up?" he said.

"I just wanted to thank you for sticking up for me," I said. "I'm sorry you got suspended."

"Don't worry about it," Nathaniel said. "What Allen did and said wasn't cool. I couldn't let him disrespect you like that."

"Was your mother mad?" I asked. Nathaniel had a brother and sister who were at least ten years older than him, so in a lot of ways he was like an only child. He already had a niece and a nephew, which I thought was really funny.

"Not really. Bree helped me explain what happened, so she was pretty cool. My momma would have been mad if I hadn't stuck up for you."

I heard Bree's voice in the background, but I couldn't make out what she was saying. I suddenly felt awkward being on the phone with Nathaniel.

"Well, I just wanted to thank you," I said. "I'll see you tomorrow…I mean, I'll see you on Friday," I corrected, remembering he wouldn't be back at school for two days.

"See you," he said and hung up.

I picked up the phone to call Aidan only to realize I didn't have his number. I remembered I had stored Nadia's number in my cell phone, so I grabbed it and gave her a call.

"Hey, Courtland," she said, answering after the second ring.

"Hey," I said. I suddenly felt strange for calling her to talk to her brother. "So how was your first day of school?"

"It was pretty interesting," she said and started laughing. "My brother must really like you if he got into a fight. I've never seen him do that."

That made me feel worse, but it was just the opening I needed. "Is he around? I wanted to thank him, you know, for sticking up for me."

"Oh, so you didn't call to talk to me?" she asked.

"Well…"

"Courtland, I'm only joking. It's cool. Aidan's not here right now, but I'll have him call you as soon as he gets back. He only ran to the store, so he should be here any minute."

"Thanks," I said.

We talked for a few more minutes, then we hung up, and I found myself pacing my room, waiting on Aidan to call. I wondered how he would sound on the phone or if he would even call me back.

When Momma called my name, I jumped and let out a little yelp. It wasn't until that moment that I realized I had been chewing on my fingernail, and Momma calling me had made me accidentally bite my finger.

"Yes," I said.

Momma didn't respond, so I answered again. When she didn't respond a second time, I knew that was my cue to go downstairs and see what she wanted.

"We decided we're going to Pizza Hut," she said.

I couldn't believe she wanted to go out when I was expecting a call from Aidan. "I thought we were going to have it delivered," I said.

"We thought it would be good to get everyone out of the house. We'll be leaving in about twenty minutes," she said.

I knew I didn't have any choice but to go, so I prayed Aidan would call me before we left. I went to the bathroom then flipped through my television channels, trying to find some way to occupy my time when I heard my cell phone chirp. I looked down and noticed I had a message, and I rushed to play it.

"Hey, Courtland, it's Aidan—Aidan Calhoun. My sister told me you called. Give me a call when you get a chance. I look forward to hearing from you." He rattled off a number and I scrambled to find some paper to write it on.

When I heard Aidan's voice, I told myself not to get excited, but I did. He sounded so good. I replayed his message a couple of times, trying to see if I could get a sense of what he was thinking, then saved it so I could listen to it later.

I nervously dialed and chewed on my nail while waiting on him to answer.

"Hello," a voice said.

I couldn't hide my disappointment that voice mail had picked up. I waited for the rest of Aidan's message so I could leave mine.

"Hello," a voice said again, and I realized it wasn't voice mail after all.

I cleared my throat, which was suddenly dry. "May I speak with Aidan?" I asked.

"Speaking."

"Hey, it's Courtland." I tried to sound casual, like we talked on the phone every day, but I wasn't sure if I pulled it off.

"Hey," he said. "Nadia told me you called. I must have just missed you. I had to run to the store for my dad."

"She told me," I said. I cleared my throat, trying to

think of what to say next, then I remembered the reason I had called. "Thank you for sticking up for me today."

"No problem," he said. "When I first heard about Allen a couple of years ago, I was really looking forward to meeting him, then when I started hearing all this stuff about him last year, I admit, I thought that first girl was lying, but then when I saw you on TV, something told me you wouldn't lie about something like that."

"You saw me on TV?" I asked.

"Yeah. That day I saw you in the mall, I had already seen you on television, and I remember thinking that I would like to get to know you. I couldn't believe it when I saw you in person."

"I'm sorry about running away. It's just that Allen has had my head kind of messed up, you know?"

"I can understand that," he said. "That guy's an idiot. He doesn't deserve you, Courtland."

Aidan's words had me on the verge of tears.

I was just about to speak when Momma walked into the room. "We're—" She took one look at me and rushed over. "What's wrong? Who are you talking to?" She tried to grab the phone from me, and I snatched it back.

"Momma, I'm fine," I said.

"Why are you crying?" she asked.

I groaned, not believing she had said it loud enough for Aidan to hear.

"Momma, I'm not crying. Something was in my eye," I said.

Momma ignored me, knowing I was lying. "Who's that on the phone?" She reached for it again.

"Momma, it's just a guy from school—the one I told you beat up Allen for me."

She brightened. "Oh, let me thank him."

I gave her a look, and I guess she realized she was messing up my game because she stepped back. "I was just coming to tell you that I'm tired, so we're not going out. I already ordered the pizza."

"Okay," I said.

"Why are you in the house talking on that cell phone? Use the house phone so you don't waste your minutes."

I sighed, embarrassed at how she was treating me. I waited until she left before I got back on the phone, wondering briefly if Aidan had hung up.

"Sorry about that," I said. "My mom can trip sometimes."

"It's just because she loves you," he said, like it was no big deal. "Did you tell her what happened?"

"Yeah," I said, then remembered what Momma had said about being on the cell phone. "Aidan, can I call you back from the house phone?" I was reaching for it as I spoke and was already dialing his number.

I heard his line beep. "That's me," I said.

He clicked over, and I hung up my cell phone. "Hey," he said, like we hadn't been talking.

"Hey," I said.

We stayed on the phone until I heard the doorbell ring about forty-five minutes later, talking about his life in

Atlanta, and how he felt about moving his senior year, which he seemed to be pretty cool with.

He told me his dad, Durwin, was an engineer in Atlanta, and he normally worked there during the week and came to Birmingham on the weekends, but he'd come to town for their first day of school. His mom, Deena, owned her own business and was opening a new location in Birmingham. I also learned he and Nadia had a little sister, Nya, who was Cory's age and was in private school at Our Lady of Fatima.

I told him a little about my family, about my dad being a police officer and my mom working at our church, as well as about Cory. I even told him about Worth the Wait and our plans for the conference and ball in the spring.

"So can guys come to the meetings?" he asked.

"Yes," I said slowly, "but we've never had one attend. Guys don't think it's cool for girls to know they're virgins."

"I think it's cool," he said.

"You're a virgin?" I asked, not believing I had come out and asked a guy something so personal. It was just that Aidan was so easy to talk to. Although I had heard him say it on TV, I wanted to make sure it wasn't just for show.

"Yep, and proud of it. I plan on being a virgin until I get married," he said.

"Me, too," I said. "When I saw you on TV—"

"Oh, so you've been checking a brother out," he said.

"You were on the news the other week, and I happened to catch it," I said. "You were talking about being a virgin and getting your college degree. I thought that was really cool, and I was hoping you weren't just saying it for the camera."

He laughed. "I guess it would be a way to draw girls," he said. "When I first started wearing my purity ring, I used to get hit on all the time because girls thought I was married. They ran the other way when I said I was a virgin, like it was a disease or something."

I couldn't help but laugh, too.

I heard a woman's voice in the background, and Aidan told me he had to go eat dinner with his family, which I thought was nice. He told me he would call me back later, and I found myself really looking forward to the call.

"So what's the name of the young man you were talking to?" Momma asked over dinner. Instead of pizza, she had ordered one of those pasta meals, which actually tasted pretty good. Luckily Cory butted in with a question about her slumber party, so I didn't answer.

Once I was done eating, I volunteered to clean up the kitchen and even took out the trash, which made Momma and Daddy look at me strangely. I was trying to do everything I could think of so they wouldn't disturb me when Aidan called me back.

"So tell me about this new guy," Momma said as I was sweeping the floor.

I kept looking at the floor. "He and his twin sister just transferred to Grover this year," I said, shrugging like it was no big deal. "His sister and I met this summer while we were at the mall, and I just wanted to show them around since it was their first day."

"That was nice of you," Momma said. Although I wasn't looking at her, I could tell she was staring at me.

"So, do you like him?" she finally asked.

"Momma, I don't even know him." I heard my voice squeak, and I tried to ignore it as I reached for a dishcloth, ran it under the faucet and swiped it over the counters, stopping to focus on an extremely difficult spot that didn't really exist.

She walked up behind me, and I turned around.

"I can tell you like him," she said. "I just want you to take things slow. Allen had us all fooled, and I just don't want to see you get hurt again."

"But Aidan is different," I said. I hadn't meant to say his name, but I realized it wouldn't be too hard for Momma to find out since there weren't any other male/female twins who were seniors at Grover, at least as far as I knew.

"I hope he is," she said. "I just don't think you need to rush into another relationship. Why don't you spend some time getting to know yourself?"

I knew Momma meant well, but something told me that Aidan really was different. I wanted to get to know him, but I didn't want Momma to worry.

"OK," I said, just to get her off my back. "I won't get into another relationship."

Even as I said the words, I found myself wondering what it would be like to be Aidan Calhoun's girl.

SIX

BY Friday, I was really looking forward to Aidan's return. We had been talking on the phone nonstop after I got home from school the last few days. I had told him what Momma said about me getting into a relationship so fast, and he told me that there was no pressure, although he made it clear he was interested in me.

I parked my car and headed for the school building, focused on getting to my locker where Aidan was supposed to meet me before homeroom. I was so intent on where I was going, I didn't realize a school bus had pulled up until I was suddenly surrounded by students. I felt a hard shove from behind, and before I knew it I was on the ground with people walking quickly all around me. Somehow I managed to roll out of the way to keep from getting trampled. I managed to lean up against a wall and struggled to catch my breath. My capri pants had a big hole at the knee, and my palms were burning from meeting with the concrete.

I was trying to figure out who had pushed me, but that became clear enough when I saw two of Allen's friends looking back at me as they laughed and slapped each other five. I thought about confronting them, but what could I really say?

By the time I made it up the stairs and down the hall to the locker I shared with Bree, my knee was throbbing, and I was walking with a limp. Bree was hugged up with Nathaniel.

"Hey," I said so they would move from in front of the locker.

"Hey," Bree said, focusing on me. "What happened to you?"

I opened the locker and looked in the mirror we had hung inside. I looked horrible. "I fell," I said. I thought about telling her the truth, but since Nathaniel was standing there, I didn't want him to get upset and go after the guys and end up getting expelled because of me.

"Are you okay?" Bree asked. "Do you need to see the nurse?"

I shook my head as I thought about going home to change clothes. I remembered I had a pair of jeans in my trunk that I was going to take back to the mall because I didn't like the way they fit, but they were better than what I had on, so I went to get them.

By the time I changed, the bell was ringing for homeroom, and I had to hurry so I wasn't late. It wasn't until Ms. Gordon was calling roll that I remembered I hadn't seen Aidan. I pulled out my phone to text him, and he texted me right back saying he'd see me during lunch, which was almost four hours away.

My classes seemed to drag that morning. By the time I made it to English, I was ready for it to be over so I could see Aidan. I slid into my desk and reached into my notebook to get my homework, smiling when I saw a copy of the invitation I had designed on the computer for Cory's slumber party, which was that evening.

She had invited three friends, and they were all coming, and Cory was so excited. I had asked Nadia and Bree. Nadia was going to Atlanta for the weekend to visit her grandparents, but Bree was planning on coming, which actually surprised me because she and Nathaniel were practically engaged as much time as they were spending with each other.

The bell had just rung when Allen came strolling in. It felt like déjà vu since he had been in my English class last year, but this time, there were no chills running up and down my spine. He slid into a chair in the back of the room, but that was still too close as far as I was concerned. I couldn't really focus knowing he was so close, and he kept making his presence known, talking loud and laughing when nothing was funny.

Why hadn't I noticed when we were dating how silly and immature he was?

When class was finally over, I rushed to gather my books and to get out of there before he could say anything to me, but I wasn't fast enough. He walked past my desk, never breaking his stride as he slid a folded piece of paper toward me. I automatically took it, but I thought twice about opening it. Finally, curiosity got the best of me, and I read the note.

I GUESS YOU'RE STUCK WITH ME, it read. He had sent me a similar note last year, and I had read it over and over after I received it. This time I tore it into tiny pieces and threw it in the trash, wanting nothing more than to never have to see Allen again.

I never knew how loud little girls could be until I attended Cory's slumber party. There were only four of them, but they talked nonstop from the moment they arrived with pillows, sleeping bags and stuffed teddy bears. Cory happily went up to her room to get her bear. She had been really worried that her friends would laugh at her if they saw it, and I told her she didn't need to worry. It made me feel good to know I was right.

They played Twister Moves and sang karaoke then settled down for some pizza, popcorn and a few episodes of *True Jackson, VP,* and *Hannah Montana* before asking me and Bree to give them makeovers. We had a good time, polishing their nails, putting their hair in these crazy styles and piling their faces with makeup that Momma insisted they wash off as soon as we were done.

By the time Bree and I headed up to my room to start our own slumber party, the girls didn't look as though they were going to sleep any time soon. Momma tried to make them go to bed, but Bree and I convinced her that the purpose of a slumber party wasn't to sleep. It was to spend time having fun with your friends.

Momma just shook her head and went upstairs where I heard her on the phone, I assumed with Daddy, who was at work.

Bree threw herself on the bed and pulled her cell phone out of her backpack.

"Who are you calling?" I asked.

She looked at me like I had asked a really silly question. "Nathaniel," she said.

I grabbed the phone from her. "I thought we agreed no phone calls to guys," I said.

"I just wanted to say good-night," she complained.

"Yeah, right," I said. "Your good-night would last for two hours."

She laughed, knowing I was right. She put the phone away and turned to face me.

"So what really happened to your leg today?" she asked.

I put my finger to my lip, indicating she should be quiet, then peeped down the hall to see if anyone was listening. I had been to enough slumber parties to know eavesdropping was a good way to pass some time. I heard the girls laughing and talking and I could barely make out Momma's voice. I pushed up the door then jumped back on the bed.

"Allen's friends pushed me," I said.

"I knew you didn't just fall," she said. "Why didn't you tell me?"

I explained about not wanting to get Nathaniel upset and she nodded in understanding.

"Have they done anything else?"

I told her about Allen's note as well as about a couple of other things that had happened that week. I didn't have proof, but something told me Allen and his friends were the ones behind me having a flat tire.

"What are you going to do?" she asked.

I shrugged, hugging a pillow close to me. "Nothing," I said. "I figure if I ignore them, they'll eventually stop."

"But what if they don't?" she asked.

I really hadn't thought about that. "I don't know."

Bree's phone rang, and I could tell from the ring tone it was Nathaniel. "Go ahead," I said.

I went downstairs to check on the girls, and two of them looked like they wouldn't be awake much longer. I got Cory and Destini some juice then looked in on Momma, who looked half-awake.

"You need anything?" I asked.

She shook her head and stifled a yawn. "No thank you, baby."

"Okay, well, I'll see you in the morning."

She nodded, sliding deeper under the covers. "Keep an eye on your sister, okay?"

"Yes, ma'am."

Bree was watching TV by the time I made it back to the room. "Aidan called you," she said, tossing me my cell phone.

I barely caught it. "Why didn't you call me?" I said, rushing to dial his number.

"Because we're not supposed to be on the phone," she reminded me.

I ignored her as Aidan picked up. "Hey," I said, trying to sound sexy, and Bree rolled her eyes. I stuck my tongue out at her. "Are you guys in Atlanta?"

"We just got here," he said, sounding tired.

"Are you staying with your grandparents?"

"Yeah. They have this huge house, so they don't even know we're here when we visit. They have an indoor basketball court, and that's all I plan to do tomorrow."

"An indoor court?" I said. "They must have serious money."

"They do," he said. "They live not too far from Tyler Perry."

"For real?" I said. I had seen most of Tyler Perry's movies, and I actually enjoyed them. I figured Aidan's grandparents had to be millionaires if they lived near him.

"You ever heard of Sweet Eats?" he asked.

"Yeah," I said. Momma and I bought their cakes and pies all the time from the grocery store. Their red velvet cake was just as good as Momma's if not better, although I would never tell her that.

"That's my grandparents' company."

"What?" I shrieked. "Your grandparents own Sweet Eats? How come you never told me?"

Bree, who had been watching a rerun of *Gossip Girl*, looked over at me, suddenly interested in my conversation.

"I told you my mom moved to start a new business," he said.

"Yeah, but apparently she owns the company." I suddenly remembered Momma saying something about a Sweet Eats opening on Highway 280. "Wait a minute, does your mother own that new Sweet Eats?"

"Yeah," he said, like it was no big deal.

I shook my head, not believing he hadn't told me.

"So why haven't you brought me any free samples?" I joked just as something else occurred to me. "Where do you live?"

"In Greystone," he murmured, like he was embarrassed he lived in one of Birmingham's richest neighborhoods.

"So how are you able to go to Grover?" I asked, knowing he should be attending a school in Hoover.

He sighed, like he really didn't want to answer. "One of the deals my dad made about us moving our senior year was that we got to pick the school we attended. Nadia didn't care, but I wanted to attend Grover because a lot of good players have come through there."

"So you used someone else's address?" I said, knowing plenty of kids who did that.

"No," he said. "My parents just know some people."

"Oh, you got a hook-up," I said, and started laughing.

Aidan had to laugh, too.

"I'm glad I did," he said. "Otherwise I wouldn't be getting to know you."

I blushed. We talked for a few more minutes, then we hung up, agreeing to talk the next day.

"Took you long enough," Bree said, never taking her eyes off *The Tyra Banks Show.*

"I know you're not talking," I said, getting up to check on the girls. They had all fallen asleep, so I turned off the TV then turned on the light in the downstairs bathroom so they would be able to find it if they had to go in the middle of the night.

"They're asleep," I said to Bree.

She grinned. "Since this is their first slumber party, let's initiate them," she said.

It didn't take me but a second to know what she was talking about. My first slumber party had been at a girl named LaTonya's house. At some point during the night, her older sister had covered each girl's face in toothpaste, and I had been doing it to new girls at every slumber party I went to after that.

I ran down the hall and grabbed a tube of toothpaste, then we tiptoed downstairs and took turns covering the girls in the stickiness. We had to bite back laughter as a couple of them scratched at their faces, spreading the toothpaste even more.

When we were done, we crept into Momma's room and covered her face, too.

It had been a while since I had had such a good time with my best friend, and I promised myself we would have to do it more often. Life just couldn't get any better.

seven

The Wednesday after Cory's slumber party, we had our first official Worth the Wait meeting of the year. Although I had been looking forward to it since I woke up that morning, by the time school was out, all I wanted to do was go home and climb in bed.

Allen and his boys were bothering me every chance they got. I had returned from lunch to find my English homework gone from my locker, although I knew I had put it there that morning because I had shown it to another kid in my class. I explained what happened, and although Ms. Merriweather seemed doubtful, she had given me until the next day to turn it in. I had seen Allen laughing a few times, so I knew he had something to do with it.

I had tried to put what happened out of my mind since I was going to see Aidan during lunch, but I hadn't been able to see him, either. As I was walking into the cafeteria, another student had been pushed toward me, and the next thing I knew, my new pink outfit was covered in spaghetti and meat sauce. Nadia had a pair of khaki pants and a white shirt she let me borrow, which was cool. Somehow I knew Allen and his boys were behind what had happened.

I had asked Nadia if she wanted to attend the Worth the Wait meeting with me, but she couldn't because she had piano lessons. Her dream was to go to Juilliard, and the way she practiced, I knew it would happen.

I was trying to decide whether I had enough time to stop by my house and get a snack before heading to my Worth the Wait meeting when Bree stopped me.

"I'm not going to be able to come to the meeting today," she said.

"Why not?" I grabbed a few books from our locker. Since the incident where my homework had come up missing, I had started carrying all my notebooks with me, but my books were too heavy to lug around all day.

"I have to go to another meeting," she said.

I wrinkled my nose, trying to recall if she had mentioned anything about it. "You're an officer," I said. "Don't you think you need to be there?"

"I know," Bree said. "I'll be at the next one. I promise."

Nathaniel walked up, and they hurried off. I looked at them holding hands and joking together as they walked down the hall, and I couldn't help but be really happy for my best friend.

Someone walked up behind me and covered my eyes, and I grinned, knowing it was Aidan.

"Hey," I said, swinging around. I frowned when I saw Allen standing behind me.

"I knew you missed me," he said, grinning.

"I thought you were someone else," I said, trying to walk around him. He stepped in front of me, blocking my path.

"Courtland, why are we playing these games? You know you want me."

The more I saw Allen lately, the more he made me sick to my stomach, and I wondered what I had ever seen in him.

"What I want is for you to leave me alone," I said.

He laughed. "Maybe I'll think about it if you do this book report for me," he said. During class, Ms. Merriweather had assigned a book report on Zora Neale Hurston's *Their Eyes Were Watching God*.

"Why don't you just watch the movie and write the report like half the kids in class are going to do?" I said.

"I don't have time," he said. He stretched and rubbed his stomach, which would have had me drooling a year ago.

"And you think I have time to do your homework?" I gave a dry laugh.

Allen grinned. "Thanks, baby," he said, talking real loud. He leaned down and kissed me, and I struggled to get free, swiping at my mouth the moment he let go.

"Are you crazy?" I screamed.

Allen didn't say a word as he walked away.

I turned around to go after him to tell him not to ever

touch me again, but I was only able to take a couple of steps because Aidan was standing there.

"You okay?" he asked.

I could only nod. I swiped at my mouth again, not believing what Allen had done. "I didn't want him to kiss me," I finally managed to say.

"I know," Aidan said. "I heard your conversation. You want me to go and say something to him? What he did wasn't cool."

I thought about Aidan getting suspended because of me, and I shook my head. "I'm sure he won't do it again."

"You're sure?" Aidan asked skeptically.

"Yeah," I said, trying to sound convincing.

"If you have any more problems, let me know," he said.

I nodded and gathered my books, then he walked me to the car.

I didn't have time to stop by the house before the Worth the Wait meeting, and I barely made it on time. We had a couple of new girls, and I took the time to greet each of them. As president, I wanted to create an atmosphere where girls felt comfortable being themselves. I wanted them to walk away from our meetings loving themselves. I was still learning that the only way a guy was going to love you and respect your decisions was if you loved yourself.

We started the meeting with prayer, then got right down to business discussing the purity conference and ball. We got updates from the committees, then we tossed around a few ideas for the actual ball, which was where each of us would be escorted by our father or some other adult male role model, and we would each sign a vow to lead a pure, unblemished life and to remain virgins until we got married.

"Do we have to be escorted by our dads?" someone asked.

"Yes," I said. "Why wouldn't they escort us?"

"I just think it would look better if we had a guy our own age escort us, like our boyfriend or something."

"This isn't a debutante ball," I said.

"But it isn't a wedding, either," Jessica Cabrera pointed out. She had contacted me over the summer about joining the group, and I could already tell she was going to have a really positive impact. She had a lot of suggestions, and had already started working on a Web site for us.

"We're going to be wearing white dresses and our fathers are going to be walking us down the aisle. It's like he's the groom. I think it's kind of weird," Felicity said.

"I never thought about it like that," I admitted.

"Well, you should," Felicity said.

We voted on who should escort us—boyfriends or fathers—and fathers won, although I think it was mainly because only a handful of girls had boyfriends. We decided we would invite our fathers to a meeting in the next month or so so we could give them an idea of what the event would be like.

After a word of prayer, we wrapped things up, and I headed home, glad the day was finally over.

As hard as I thought, I couldn't figure out a way to get Allen and his friends to leave me alone, so it was a relief when I went a few days with nothing happening. I was lying across the bed watching an old episode of *Daddy's Girls* after school one day when Momma came into the room.

"We're leaving in a few minutes," she said, standing in my door as she struggled to put on an earring.

"Where are we going?" I asked.

Momma looked at me like I was crazy. "Did they not mention open house at school today?"

I groaned. "You're actually going to that?"

"Don't I go every year?" she asked.

"That's my point," I said, sitting up. "Nothing changes. It's always the same boring message from the principal and meetings with the teachers. You already know I'm doing well in school."

"I'm still going," she said.

"Well, do I have to go?"

Momma just looked at me for a few seconds, and I knew that meant I needed to get moving.

When I got downstairs, Daddy and Cory were waiting by the door.

"You're going?" I asked. Although Cory normally went with us, it had been years since Daddy had been to an open house.

Cory nodded, looking excited at the thought.

"Are you sure taking Cory is a good idea?" I asked Momma. "A lot of students might be there." We hadn't told Cory that Allen was still at Grover, and although I wanted to protect my sister, part of me dreaded the thought of my whole family rolling up to school with me. It was just too much.

Momma hesitated for a minute. "It will be fine," she finally said.

We all piled into Momma's Honda Pilot and headed to Grover. The school really looked pretty all lit up. The place was packed. Principal Abernathy was standing at the door greeting parents, and there was a table set up near the auditorium with cookies and punch.

I looked around, grinning when I spotted Bree and Nathaniel.

"Can I sit with them?" I asked.

"No," Daddy said. "We're sitting together."

"Can I at least go over and say hello?" I said with an attitude.

When they didn't respond, I glanced at Bree and shook my head, letting her know I couldn't sit with her, then waved at her mother, Ms. Davis, who called me over and gave me a hug.

We headed into the auditorium, and I flopped into a chair.

"Sit up," Momma said, and I rolled my eyes as I straightened up in my chair just as the lights were lowered. I looked around in surprise, wondering what to expect.

A projection screen lowered from the ceiling and a slide show began. There were photos of all the teachers, which I hoped meant Principal Abernathy wasn't going to turn around and introduce all of them.

When they started showing various shots of students from school, kids started cheering for the popular kids. When a photo of me, which had to have been taken last year since I was wearing my cheerleading uniform, popped up, there were a lot of boos.

"Courtland Murphy is a liar. She slept with my boy Allen Benson and she slept with me, too," someone yelled. It had to be a guy because the voice was really deep.

Principal Abernathy immediately brought the slideshow to an end. I tried to ignore people bursting out laughing. The whole thing probably didn't last a minute, but it felt longer than all the years I had been in school combined.

I sat there speechless, not believing what had happened. People were whispering, and even in the darkness I could feel people staring at me.

I got up and ran out of the auditorium, glad I was seated on the end of the row. I had barely made it outside when I felt someone behind me. It wasn't until I was wrapped in her arms that I realized it was Momma.

"Baby, are you okay?" she asked.

I couldn't even speak I was so humiliated. Tears streamed down my face, and I struggled to catch my breath. "Why would they say those things?" I asked. "I dropped the charges against Allen. He can still get a basketball scholarship. Why won't they just leave me alone?"

Instead of responding, Momma led me outside to our car.

It was a few minutes before Daddy showed up with Cory, and I don't think I had ever seen him that mad. Cory just looked confused.

He turned and looked at me. "Are you okay?" he asked quietly.

I just nodded, still too upset to speak.

"Why would someone say all those mean things about you?" Cory asked.

That just made me cry harder.

"Because boys have nothing better to do. I can't believe their parents put up with that foolishness," Momma fussed as she wrapped me in her arms and rocked me. Daddy just sat there looking like he was going to kill somebody.

"Have they been bothering you?" he asked.

I nodded.

"What have they been doing?"

Somehow I managed to list everything that had happened since school started, trying not to scare Cory when I mentioned Allen.

"Why didn't you say something?" Momma asked.

I didn't respond because I noticed a few people leaving the school. "Can we go?" I asked.

Daddy started the car without a word, and we drove home in silence.

Although she didn't want to, my parents made Cory go to bed as soon as we walked through the door.

"You're changing schools," Momma said when we were alone, and I looked horrified.

"Momma, you promised I could stay at Grover. It's my last year," I whined.

"We can't have these guys harassing you," Momma said. "I can't believe someone said those things. Where were their parents?"

I didn't remind her she had already asked those questions. "I don't want to change schools," I said.

"Why would you want to stay at a school where people say such horrible things about you—unless those things are true?"

I was too hurt even to respond to what Momma had said.

She looked like she wanted to say something else, but Daddy spoke instead. "It's been a long night, and we're all tired," he said. "Let's just talk about this in the morning."

I headed upstairs, and the minute I got in my room and closed the door I texted Bree. She called me back within seconds.

"Was everybody talking?" I asked.

"A few people were," she said, but I knew she was just being nice.

"What where they saying?" I asked.

"That's not important," she said, which made me groan. I knew that meant I had been the talk of open house.

"Did you see Aidan? What did he say?" I asked.

"They didn't come," she said. "Nadia texted me to let me know they had to go to Atlanta because their grandmother was rushed to the hospital."

"Is she okay?" I asked. I really was concerned about Aidan's grandma, but I was glad to know the guy I liked hadn't seen me be humiliated in front of the whole school yet again. I ignored the fact I was finally admitting to myself that I liked Aidan.

That Friday when I walked into school, the air was filled with excitement. Our first football game of the year would be that night, and as I entered the building, I smiled at the colorful posters the cheerleaders and pep squad had used to decorate the school. It kind of made me sad because last year, since I was part of the squad, I had helped with the decorations. Rene White was now captain, and she couldn't have been happier. I still didn't like her because she always saw the negative in everything.

I had to admit, despite being embarrassed at open house, I was pretty happy these days, too. My parents had reluctantly agreed to let me stay at Grover, basketball tryouts would be happening soon, Worth the Wait was going to have a great year and...

As though reading my thoughts, Aidan appeared, giving me this sexy smile.

"Hey, Courtland."

"Hey," I said, knowing I probably sounded out of breath.

We stood there just staring at each other a few seconds

before I glanced at the floor, wondering why I was suddenly so shy. We never ran out of things to talk about on the phone.

"Are you going to the game tonight?" he finally asked.

I looked at him and realized he was even cuter up close.

I nodded, scared if I spoke I would say something crazy.

"You want to go with me?"

I followed my heart and said yes, but then my head jumped in, reminding me that Momma didn't want me dating anyone so soon after Allen.

"No," I said.

Aidan, who had a big smile plastered across his face after I responded yes, frowned.

"No?"

"Yes...I mean no."

Aidan looked just as confused as I felt.

I took a deep breath then focused on him. "I really want to go with you, but my mom doesn't want me dating right now, remember?"

He nodded in understanding. "Maybe she would change her mind if I talked to her," he said.

"No, that would only make it worse," I rushed to say. "Allen did the same thing. He had us all fooled, and Momma would be suspicious if you did that."

"I'm not Allen," he said.

He looked really hurt, which made me feel horrible.

"I know," I said. The way he was responding made

me like him even more. "What about if we just meet at the game?"

"I don't like the idea of sneaking behind your parents' backs," he said. " That's not how my parents raised me. Besides, I haven't done anything wrong. I think if I introduce myself to them and explain what I'm about, they would let us date."

"Maybe in a few months, but not right now," I said. "That stuff that happened with Allen is still too new." An image of open house flashed in my head. "Please, can't we just meet at the game?"

He looked like he wanted to say no. "I really want to go out with you, Aidan. Trust me, if I thought my parents would understand, I would leave school right now so you could go meet them. My parents are really protective of me. Now that my dad has taken more interest in what I'm doing, he's worse than my mom."

Aidan laughed. "My dad's the same way about my sisters."

"Aidan, I really like you. Just trust me, okay?" I said as the bell rang, signaling it was time to get to homeroom.

He grinned. "Maybe," he said. "We can talk more tonight at the game."

I couldn't concentrate in any of my classes because I was so busy thinking about my first date with Aidan. I caught him checking me out a few times during the pep rally, but I pretended I was really into the cheerleaders' performance, which wasn't half as good as the one my cocaptain, Candy, and I had done last year.

By the time school was over, I couldn't wait to get home and change. I picked up Cory, half listening as she talked about some project she had done in class that day.

When we got home, I was relieved to see Daddy's car gone. I had mentioned the possibility of going to the game to Momma, but now that I knew I was definitely going, I had to convince her to let me drive rather than having her drop me off, which she normally liked to do if I would be late coming in.

"Hey, Momma," I said, hoping the fried tilapia she was cooking wouldn't have my hair smelling like fish when I arrived at the game.

She looked up at me and smiled. "Hey, babies," she said, looking at me and Cory. "How was school?"

I waited until Cory had finished talking and had gone upstairs to change clothes before I mentioned the game.

"Is Bree going with you?" she asked after I was done.

"I don't think she's going," I said. "I was just going to drive."

Momma was shaking her head before I could finish. "I don't think that's a good idea," she said. "It will be late when you leave, and I don't want you driving by yourself. I'll drop you off."

I was glad Momma's back was to me as she transferred the fish to a paper-towel-covered plate because I looked at her like she was crazy. "Momma," I whined, "I'm a senior in high school."

"And you'll be a senior in high school who's staying home if you don't watch your tone."

She turned around and looked at me, and I shut up real fast.

Momma sighed, looking tired. "I would feel more comfortable if you went with someone. Can you just do this for me?"

"Okay," I said, trying to think of who to call. Nadia immediately popped into my head.

I raced upstairs and immediately called her. The phone only rang one time before she picked up. "Hello."

"Girl, I need a favor," I said, figuring my name would have popped up on her caller ID.

"What's up?" she said.

"I need you to pick me up for the game."

"Okay," she said, not even hesitating, "but you know Aidan's riding with me."

I groaned, realizing I was going to have to lie to my parents so they didn't think Aidan was there to see me. "I'll be ready," I finally said. "What time will you be here?"

"Six."

"Okay," I said, glancing at my clock. It was only four, so I could chill for a minute.

I pulled out the jeans and Grover T-shirt I had decided to wear, then went downstairs to finish helping Momma with dinner. After we ate, I cleaned up the kitchen, and Momma smiled her thanks before heading upstairs to lie down.

After showering and getting dressed, I told Momma

and Cory goodbye then headed outside to wait for Nadia and Aidan. I groaned when Daddy pulled up, praying he would go inside before my friends arrived.

"Hey, Daddy," I said, meeting him at his car.

"Hey, baby," he said. "Where are you headed?"

I told him about the game, and I was glad when he looked a little distracted.

"How's your mother?" he said.

I realized this was my chance to get him inside and took it. "She didn't look like she was feeling too well," I said.

He nodded and hurried toward the front door. "Have a good time," he threw over his shoulder.

I breathed a sigh of relief as I sat down on the front step. I was only there about five minutes before Aidan and Nadia showed up in her Volkswagen Jetta.

"Hey," I said, jogging over to the car as Aidan got out.

He grinned when he saw me, and I had to laugh because although we hadn't planned it, we were dressed alike.

"I like your outfit," he said.

"I like yours, too." I blushed.

"Are your parents home?" he asked, already knowing the answer since both cars were in the driveway.

"Yeah, but my mother's not feeling well."

He looked doubtful.

"I'm serious, Aidan. She went to lie down, and my daddy went to check on her."

"If we're going to go together, Courtland, I'm going to meet your parents."

"I didn't know we were going together," I said, really liking the thought.

"Well, you know now," he said.

"Oh, give me a break," Nadia said, and we all laughed.

Aidan climbed into the backseat, and he looked surprised but pleased when I hopped back there with him.

"Oh, now I'm a chauffeur," Nadia complained.

"To the game, Charles," Aidan said in this phony British accent.

We all laughed again as we pulled off.

Nadia threw in an Alicia Keys CD and was in her own world, studying the songs as though she were preparing for the ACT. That was fine with me. Aidan grabbed my hand and I smiled at him.

"You know I really like you, right?" he said.

"I like you, too." Aidan really was a great guy—the kind of guy I had thought Allen was when I'd first met him. I shook my head, determined I wasn't going to focus on how that had turned out. Aidan was nothing like Allen.

"I was joking when I said it earlier, but I really was serious about you being my girlfriend, Courtland. I was going to ask you after the game tonight."

"You were?" I said.

"Yeah. I would be honored if you would be my girlfriend."

His words melted my heart. "I would like that a lot, Allen."

I looked up, horrified, praying I had not said my ex-boyfriend's name to the guy I wanted to be my new boyfriend. I stared at him, waiting to see how he was going to respond.

It took him a second to say, "Aren't you going to say something?"

I breathed a sigh of relief that he hadn't heard me. "I would really like that," I said, much louder than I needed to.

Nadia turned down the radio. "What?" she asked, glancing up at us in the rearview mirror. Neither Aidan nor I spoke, too busy grinning at each other. She finally got the hint and turned up the music again.

Aidan and I sat as close to each other as possible for the rest of the ride, not really saying much, but that was fine with me. Even though I hadn't been looking, I had met an amazing guy who liked me just as much as I liked him. This was definitely turning out to be the best night of my life.

It was about five minutes before the game was supposed to start by the time we made it to the football stadium. There was a sea of blue and gold, and music filled the air as Grover battled musically with our opponents the Ramsay Rams. When Aidan grabbed my hand, I couldn't help but smile. We headed toward the stands, stopping to speak to a few people along the way. A few people looked at me strangely, probably surprised to see me and Aidan together, but I didn't care.

We were just about to take a seat when I glanced at the field as the players made their way from the locker room. A couple of people on the field struggled to unfurl the banner that the team members would burst through, and I smiled, remembering the sign we had made for the first game last year. It had taken us about two weeks to make, but it was worth the effort when we saw how much the crowd liked it. One of the members of the squad was an incredible artist, and she had drawn a picture of the team along with the mascot. It had looked so real and been so pretty we had seriously thought about not letting the team burst through it.

I wondered if Rene, who didn't have a creative bone in her body, had done the same thing. To my surprise, when the banner was fully opened and on display for the entire stadium to see, I saw my face staring back at me. I did a double take, knowing I had to be wrong, but I wasn't. It was definitely the picture I had had taken for last year's yearbook. Right next to the picture, someone had written For a Good Time, Call Courtland, and had included my cell-phone number.

The words seemed to register with everyone at the same time. The whispers rushed over me like a wave, and I felt myself drowning in humiliation. Even Aidan grabbing my hand and squeezing it didn't offer much comfort.

I was too embarrassed to watch kickoff after Principal Abernathy marched onto the field and promised to punish everyone involved in the prank. Even though the announcer tried to recover as the players ran onto the field, the damage was already done. Part of me wanted to pretend I wasn't affected by the sign, but deep inside, I was really hurting. Why were these guys—I had no doubt it was Allen's friends—being so mean to me? I had dropped all the charges, and I was trying to move on with my life.

I didn't realize I was crying until Nadia leaned over and asked, "Are you okay? Do you want to leave?"

I nodded.

"You guys go to the car. I'll be there in a minute," Aidan said. He looked angrier than he had on the first day of school when Allen had spat on me, and I was scared to see what would happen if he found out who was responsible for the sign.

"No," I said, grabbing his arm. "I'm not going to the car unless you come with me."

He ignored me, looking instead at his sister. "Take her to the car."

Nadia didn't respond as she took my hand and pulled me up off the metal bleacher. She ignored my protests and led me to the car where we waited for a few minutes before Aidan showed up and calmly climbed in the backseat next to me. "You won't be having any more problems," he said, and I really believed him.

We rode around until it was time for the game to be over, and I tried to convince Aidan not to say anything to my parents. He wasn't hearing it, though. When I got home and saw Daddy's car was gone, I was relieved. Aidan insisted on coming inside anyway, figuring

Momma was home, but she was asleep, and there was a note saying Daddy and Cory had gone to the movies.

Aidan looked a little disappointed.

"Are you sure you're okay?" he asked, staring directly into my eyes.

"No," I said, surprising myself at my honesty. "I don't get why they won't leave me alone. It was bad enough they humiliated me in front of my parents...." I stopped talking, realizing he didn't know about that—or at least I hoped he didn't.

"What are you talking about?" he said.

I told him about the incident at open house, and he was hot.

"Why didn't you tell me?" he yelled.

"Because I didn't want you acting like this," I said.

We must have been louder than I realized because suddenly Momma appeared in the entryway where we were standing, catching us both by surprise.

"What's going on?" she asked, looking wide-awake. "Who are you, and why are you yelling at my daughter?"

Momma stepped in front of me protectively as Aidan tried to explain.

"Good evening, Mrs. Murphy," he said, reaching out to shake her hand.

Momma hesitated for a second before shaking his hand. "Who are you?" she repeated.

"My name is Aidan Calhoun. I go to school with your daughter."

"Oh, it's you," she said dryly, looking at me. "My daughter isn't supposed to be dating. She said a friend was picking her up."

I didn't know whether I was more embarrassed at Momma letting on I had been talking about Aidan to her or at the way she was treating him.

"His sister Nadia picked me up," I explained. "She's in the car."

Momma didn't even bother to look outside, focusing on Aidan. "Why are you in my house?"

"Momma," I said, not believing she was being so rude.

Aidan told Momma what had happened at the football game, which embarrassed me even more.

"Are you okay?" she asked, turning to examine me.

I nodded. "Aidan and Nadia were really great."

Momma turned to Aidan. "Thank you for looking out for my daughter."

"I'm glad I was there, ma'am. I really care about Courtland. I asked her to be my girlfriend tonight, and she said yes." He looked like he had won the lottery.

Momma, on the other hand, looked as though her best friend had died. "Really?" she said, looking at me. I know she was silently asking me if I had forgotten about the conversation we'd had about me not having a boyfriend.

"Yes," I said. "I really like Aidan, and I want to be his girlfriend." I had never been surer of anything else. I smiled at him, and he smiled back at me before we both turned to look at Momma. I figured since we were so sure we wanted to be together, she would give in, but I was wrong.

"Aidan, I'm sure you're a nice young man, although I couldn't tell it by the way I heard you yelling at my daughter tonight."

"I apologize, ma'am. I wasn't yelling at Courtland. I was yelling about the situation. She told me what happened at open house, and I just got upset. Courtland told me everything that happened with Allen, and you have my word, I would never treat her that way. I like her and respect her too much for that."

"That might be true," Momma said, "but I don't think it's a good idea for Courtland to have a boyfriend right now. Courtland can't see you anymore."

eight

IN the span of a few hours, I went from being the happiest girl in the world to the most disappointed. I'm pretty sure not many girls had had their mother break up with their boyfriend for them. I had been humiliated twice in one day.

The workload at school really started picking up over the next few days, but I didn't mind because I knew the spring semester would be pretty laid-back. Besides, the work helped to keep my mind off Aidan. Even though he wanted to respect Momma's decision that we not see each other, I convinced him that we could still go together, even if it was only at school.

I finished my book report, and I had turned it in the day before. Allen had been surprisingly calm when he realized I hadn't done his report for him. Maybe it was because one of the girls he had his arm wrapped around volunteered to do it for him.

I got to school the next morning after being up half

the night working on a history project, wanting nothing more than to go back to bed. I went to grab books for my first couple of classes, which were on the third floor, realizing I had time to stop by the lunchroom for breakfast. Momma hadn't been feeling well that morning, so I hadn't eaten, and my stomach was protesting.

As I grabbed my books, I realized I hadn't talked to Bree in a couple of days, so I decided to scribble her a message on the white board we had hanging up in our locker. I reached into the little basket for the marker we kept there along with a couple of pens and pencils and yanked my hand back when it came in contact with something furry.

Curious more than anything, I reached for the basket and peered inside, wondering if something had gone moldy, since, on occasion, Bree and I had been known to leave food in our lockers, even though we weren't supposed to.

This definitely was not food.

Inside the basket was a dead mouse staring blankly back at me. I dropped the basket and ran off down the hall screaming, not caring if people were looking at me like I had lost my mind. I guess a few other kids got a look at what was inside because some of them started yelling, too. I peeked from around the corner where I was hiding and watched as a teacher went over to inspect the basket. He carefully picked it up and took it outside as I tried to keep down the juice I had drunk.

The crowd continued to stand around my locker

talking, and when Bree walked up with Nathaniel, someone filled her in on what happened. She looked like she was about to throw up, too.

After finding out Bree and I shared the locker, the teacher who had disposed of the mouse suggested we go to the office and get a new locker, which was fine with me. It wasn't until we were headed to our new one near the cafeteria and I noticed some of Allen's friends laughing and pretending to scream as they looked at something in one of their lockers that I realized they had been responsible for the mouse.

I was about to walk over, prepared to tell them off, but Bree stopped me.

"Don't give them the satisfaction," she said.

"They're taking this too far," I said.

"I know, but if you say something to them, it's only going to get worse. We have to find another way to get back at them."

I nodded, knowing she was right. I wanted more than anything for all the madness to stop. The question was how to make it happen. I decided I would ask the members of Worth the Wait since in the past they had given me some really good advice.

About two weeks later, I was really looking forward to attending the Worth the Wait meeting. I had had to miss the last couple of meetings because of basketball tryouts. Coach Abrams was working us hard, but after playing all summer, I was confident I would make the team.

We had had our final tryout the day before our second Worth the Wait meeting in October, and the results were supposed to be posted on Thursday. I grabbed my backpack and other stuff that Wednesday, prepared to head to the meeting, but I stopped short when I saw the crowd gathered around my car. Kids were pointing and laughing as I made my way through the crowd, anger and fear overwhelming me when I stood in front of my green Toyota Tercel.

At least, it used to be green.

Someone had covered my car from bumper to bumper with all kinds of madness. There were words calling me out my name. I just stood in shock for a few seconds, not believing what I was seeing. When I felt someone standing beside me, I didn't even bother to look over.

"Who did this?" someone said in a quiet voice.

If I hadn't looked over, I wouldn't have known it was Aidan. The last time I had seen him so angry was the football game when he'd promised me Allen wouldn't bother me again.

"I don't know," I said. I didn't add that I had a pretty good idea of who was behind it. I'm sure a lot of other kids in the crowd did, too, since it was broad daylight, and someone had to have seen something.

Nadia and Bree made their way through the crowd, and they looked just as shocked as I felt.

"We need to call your dad," Bree finally said.

I nodded. When I didn't move, Bree reached into my purse and grabbed my cell phone, scrolling through the numbers until she came across one for my daddy. I circled my car, half listening as she tried to get in touch with him.

"He didn't answer his cell. They're trying to reach him at work," Bree said, flipping the phone closed. "He took the afternoon off, but when I told them it was an emergency, they said they'd try to get in touch with him. They're going to send someone else over if they don't get in touch with him."

I didn't bother to respond as I focused on my car.

Aidan walked over to me. "You okay?" he asked.

Something about the way he asked made me start crying. He pulled me to him and wrapped me in a tight hug, which only made me cry even harder.

"It's okay," he said.

I really wanted to believe him, but I didn't. What had I done so wrong that someone would want to damage my car? Allen had tried to rape me, and after I had pressed charges, I knew people were angry, but angry enough to mess up my car?

Aidan held me until I finally stopped crying, then he stepped back and searched my eyes, making sure I was really okay. I gave him a watery smile, and he seemed satisfied.

When a police car pulled up, I felt a little better, realizing my daddy had finally shown up, but it wasn't my daddy. It was some guy I had never seen before. By then, the crowd had died down, but Aidan, Nadia, Bree and Nathaniel had stuck around, mainly to make sure I was okay.

The officer took down the report, then circled my car. "Why don't you try and start it?" he suggested.

I slid behind the wheel and, out of habit, buckled my seat belt, checked my rearview mirror, then my sideview.

I turned the key in the ignition and listened in relief as the engine came to life...then died.

"You'll need to call a tow truck," he said. "Sounds like your battery's dead."

"Do you think a mechanic can fix it?" I asked hopefully. He nodded.

As we stood waiting for the tow-truck driver to show up, Bree took pictures of the car with her camera phone in case we needed them for the insurance company.

I had turned around to ask her a question when I saw a car drive past with Allen in the passenger seat. He gave me this weird smile, then the car sped away, and if I had had any doubts before, they were all erased. Allen had trashed my car—or he knew who had done it.

I tried calling my parents again, but neither one answered their cell phones. Finally, after the tow truck left, Aidan offered to drive me home.

"Are you sure you're okay?" Nadia asked as she was about to climb into the backseat of Aidan's old Mustang.

"Yeah," I said, but really I wasn't. All I was trying to do was move on with my life, and Allen and his stupid friends wouldn't even let me do that.

It took me a long time to fall asleep that night. The more I thought about the way I was being treated, the worse I felt. Before I could stop myself, I snatched up my cell phone and called Allen, ready to go off.

When his phone went straight to voice mail, I hung up in frustration. Finally, I texted him: Leave me alone.

I didn't know if it would help, but it did make me feel a little better. I waited about an hour for him to respond, but when no message came back, I finally went to bed.

When I woke up the next morning, the house was really quiet and the sun was barely peeking through my bedroom window. I glanced over at my clock and realized it was only six, so I rolled over hoping I could fall back asleep. Finally, about fifteen minutes later, I got up and, after stopping by the bathroom, went downstairs. Momma was already up, doing her morning devotion.

Momma must have heard me coming, because she glanced up at me and smiled.

"What are you doing up so early?" she asked.

I shrugged. "I couldn't sleep."

"Upset about what happened yesterday or nervous about finding out whether you made the team?" She patted a spot next to her, and I plopped down on the sofa and leaned my head on her shoulder. She dropped a kiss on my forehead and rubbed my hair, which she used to do when I was little.

With everything that had happened the day before, I had forgotten about basketball tryouts.

"Why does he hate me, Momma?" I asked. "I'm just trying to move on with my life. I could have pressed charges, but I didn't. I just don't get it."

Momma wrapped her arms around me. "I don't know why Allen won't leave you alone, baby. I was praying about that before you came down."

She took a deep breath, and I turned to look at her, knowing I wasn't going to like what she said.

"I would really feel better if you changed schools," she said.

"Momma, you promised," I whined. "It's my senior year."

"This thing with Allen doesn't look like it's getting any better. I'm just worried he'll do something crazy."

She didn't say it, but I know she was thinking about the fact that Allen had run over Aunt Dani and left her in a parking lot, not knowing whether she was dead or alive. If he had done that to her, what would he do to me?

Suddenly I was scared. More and more, I was seeing a side of Allen I didn't like, and, as much as I wanted to be free from him, I wasn't. The things he had done to me so far were embarrassing, but what if they got worse? What if he tried to kill me or to hurt someone in my family?

I knew I couldn't let that happen. The way I saw it, I only had to get through about two more months. By then the semester would be over and Allen would be out of my life for good—I hoped. What could I do to keep him from tormenting me in the meantime though?

The question was on my mind all day at school, and it wasn't until the end of the day that it occurred to me what I needed to do. The only reason Allen was causing trouble was because it was obvious I didn't want him. When we were together, I didn't have any problems out of him or his friends, so maybe if we got back together all the madness would stop.

I smiled to myself, realizing it was a great plan. The timing was perfect because with basketball season starting, I could pretend I needed his help. I hurried to the gym to check out the list of people who had made the team. There were only a couple of people hanging around the list, and I grinned to myself, anticipating seeing my name.

After checking the list three times, my grin faded. My name was nowhere to be found.

I checked again, sure there had to be some kind of mistake. Things had gone well during tryouts, and I had been sure there was going to be a spot for me on the team. Actually, I thought I was going to be starting.

I headed to Coach Abrams's office, suddenly not caring about my next class.

"Do you have a minute?" I asked when he looked up from his computer.

He looked like he wanted to say no, but I didn't give him a chance.

"Can you tell me why I didn't make the team?" I asked, stepping into his office.

He shrugged. "Not really."

"Not really?" I asked. Part of me couldn't believe how bold I was being, but I really wanted to know. "Was it my skills? Is there something I need to improve?"

"Your skills were fine, Murphy," he said.

"Then why didn't I make the team?"

He walked over to his door, looked up and down the hall then closed the door.

"Murphy, you're a talented player, but putting you on the team would be a major distraction for the other players."

My mouth dropped open, not believing what I was hearing. "What?" I whispered.

He gave a dry laugh. "Look, I don't have time for drama on my team. I'm planning on going to the championship this year, and I need all my players to focus. You're a good player, but I don't think your head will be in the game. I can give you a spot on the team, but you'll ride the bench all season."

His words made me angry, and before I could stop myself, I went off. "What do you mean my head won't be in the game?"

I was so mad I couldn't breathe. Suddenly I was tired. It wasn't worth fighting anymore. I turned around and walked out of his office without another word.

Before I could stop myself I was out of the school building and heading home. My daddy didn't even look surprised when he saw me. I guess my expression told him everything he needed to know.

"What happened?" he asked, leaving his chair in the living room to meet me at the door.

The words just poured out of me. I told him everything that had happened with the coach and what Allen and his friends had been doing to me. I even told him about my plan to pretend to like Allen again to see if that would make them stop. He just listened, just like he used to do when I was little.

When I was finally done, he handed me a tissue.

"So what do you want to do?" he asked quietly.

"I don't know," I wailed. "I just want all this to stop."

"Do you want me to talk to them?" he asked.

"Who?"

"Allen, the coach, Allen's friends, whoever you want me to talk to."

I started to say no, but then I realized that maybe it would be good to have Daddy's help. "You're not going to hurt anybody, are you?" I asked, really worried he would.

He laughed. "I hope it won't come to that, but if it does…" He shrugged.

"Daddy," I said, drawing it out like it had ten syllables.

"These guys need to know you have family who love you and who aren't going to stand for any nonsense. That's why Allen got away with as much as he did. I wasn't as involved as I should have been, and now you're paying for it."

"It's okay, Daddy," I said.

"No, it's not," he said. "I promise if I can help it, no one will ever hurt you again." He glanced at his watch then gave me a hug. "I have to get out of here," he said. "How come you were home in the middle of the day?" He had changed his shift a few months ago, and for the most part he worked days, unless he was working overtime.

"I left something at home," he said. "Why don't you go take a nap?"

"You're not mad at me about leaving school?" I asked. Momma and Daddy didn't play when it came to our education.

"Everybody needs to take a day every now and then. Just don't make it a habit." He kissed me on the forehead and headed out the door.

I fixed myself a grilled ham-and-cheese sandwich then headed upstairs to my room. I lay awake for a while thinking about the last few months and hoping now that Daddy was going to get involved it was finally going to come to an end.

The sound of the doorbell awakened me. I sat up abruptly and glanced at the clock. It was three in the afternoon. I headed downstairs still half-asleep just as someone started pounding on the door.

"I'm coming," I yelled and snatched the door open.

Bree was standing there looking worried. "What took you so long?" she asked, brushing past me. "I've been outside for five minutes."

"How'd you get here?" I asked.

"I drove today."

"Where's Nathaniel?" They were practically joined at the hip, so I was surprised he wasn't lurking outside.

"I told him we needed to take a break," she said matter-of-factly.

I looked at her like she was crazy. "Why?"

Suddenly Bree's cheerful facade crumbled. "I know you have a lot going on, but I really need to talk to you," she said.

Something about her words scared me. I led her into the den and plopped beside her on the sofa. "What's wrong?" I asked.

Bree sat staring at the floor. "Why'd you leave school early?" she asked.

"I didn't make the team," I said. "Stop stalling. What's wrong?"

Bree took a deep breath then looked at me. "I think I'm pregnant."

I started laughing. "Girl, why would you think something like that? To be pregnant you'd have to be having se..." My eyes grew big as the realization hit me. "You've been having sex and you didn't tell me?"

She smiled through watery eyes. "What exactly was I supposed to say?"

There were a thousand questions running through my head, but I knew I would have to wait to ask them. I focused on my best friend and what she had said. "What makes you think you're pregnant?"

"I haven't had a period in, like, two months, I'm throwing up every five minutes, and my breasts hurt," she said, rubbing one then wincing to emphasize her point.

"Have you taken a test?" I asked.

She shook her head. "I'm scared," she said. "Courtland, what if I'm pregnant? I'm seventeen. I can't have a baby."

I hugged her and let her cry just like Daddy had done for me earlier. Before I could stop myself, I found myself saying, "Why didn't you use a condom? Did you guys get tested before you started having sex? What if Nathaniel has AIDS or something?" I realized as soon as the words came out that they were the wrong thing to say, but it was too late to take them back. Bree cried even harder.

I knew I had to take control of the situation. "Come on," I said, helping her up.

"Where are we going?" she asked as she followed me.

"We have to find out for sure."

We headed first to Wal-Mart, but I remembered a few months earlier when I had gone in there and almost been busted by our adviser, Andrea, looking at condoms. I figured it would be too easy for someone who knew us to be in Wal-Mart, so instead I headed to Walgreens. With a boldness I didn't feel, I marched into the store while Bree waited in the car, and I grabbed the first pregnancy test box I saw. I glanced and saw it had two kits in the box, which I thought might come in handy. After I paid for it, I hurried out and breathed a sigh of relief when I was safely in the car.

We decided to go back to my house, and Bree had just gone into the bathroom when Momma came home.

"Hey, Momma," I said, knowing I was talking loud, trying to hint to Bree to pretend everything was normal. "Hey, Cory."

"Hey, baby," Momma said, looking tired.

Cory waved and headed upstairs. "Bree's in the bathroom," I yelled, figuring that's where she was going. I could hear Cory heading to the bathroom in Momma and Daddy's room.

"How is Bree?" Momma asked.

"Fine. She just came over to hang out for a while."

She nodded. "I'm not feeling well, so I'm going to go lie down. Can you go pick up something to eat? Just get my debit card out of my purse."

"Okay. I hope you feel better."

By the time I got back upstairs, Bree was sitting on my bed and, without seeing the actual pregnancy test, I knew.

nine

I grabbed Bree and held her as tight as I could as tears streamed down my face.

"We have to go to the doctor," I said. "Sometimes those tests are wrong."

"Courtland, I took both of them," she said. "They both came out positive."

"Still, we have to be sure." I tried to sound upbeat, but I really wasn't feeling it. My best friend was pregnant. She knew it, and as much as I wanted to pretend otherwise, I knew it, too.

We sat in silence for a few minutes, and although neither of us said it, I'm sure we were both thinking the same thing: how much Bree's life was going to change.

"I'd better go," she said. She grabbed her cell phone and called Nathaniel, and although they talked for a few minutes, I was still in shock, so I didn't pay much attention.

"What are you going to do?" I asked.

She shrugged. "I don't know. Keep it, I guess."

I nodded. "I'll help you," I said. "It's going to be all right." Even as I said the words, I wondered if it really was going to be. Bree was only seventeen. How was she going to handle going to school and having a baby?

After she left, I lay across my bed, not believing what had happened. How did I not know my best friend was having sex? How did I miss the signs of her being pregnant? Maybe it was just my imagination, but she did look different.

I laughed at myself. That was something that people my mother's age said. Maybe Bree just looked different because I expected her to.

"Courtland, Momma wants you to go pick up dinner," Cory said from my doorway. Her sudden appearance scared me, and before I knew it I was yelling at her.

"Can't you knock?" I screamed.

She looked really surprised, and I could tell by the way she started blinking her eyes behind her glasses that she was about to cry.

"I'm sorry, Cory," I said. "I've got a lot on my mind right now."

"Were you thinking about Allen?" she said.

"No," I snapped. I took a deep breath, not wanting to go off on her. "Look, can you just leave me alone?"

"But what about dinner?" she asked.

"I'll take care of it," I said. "Now, could you please leave?"

Cory looked like she was going to say something

else, but she changed her mind and turned and walked off. She was back a few minutes later, which annoyed me even more.

"What?" I asked, not caring that I sounded irritated.

She threw a debit card on the floor. "Momma told me to give you this," she said. "She wants beef and broccoli from Formosa's, and she said to tell them to make it extra spicy."

I snatched the card and left without another word. I just needed to get out of the house and clear my head. It wasn't until I got to the Chinese restaurant that I realized I didn't know what everybody else wanted.

Momma answered on the second ring. After giving me the rest of the order, she turned serious. "We need to talk when you get home."

"Can't you tell me now?" I asked. "Hang on." I placed my order then refocused on our conversation. "We can talk now. It will be ten minutes before the order is ready."

"No, I'd rather discuss this in person."

Something about her tone told me she knew about Bree. "Okay. I'll see you in a few."

"Be careful," she said.

"I will." I rushed off the phone, trying to figure out how she had found out when suddenly it hit me that Bree had probably left the pregnancy test in the bathroom. I groaned, not believing I hadn't thought to empty the trash.

The whole ride home, I tried to figure out what I was going to say to Momma. Although I knew I hadn't done anything wrong, I felt really guilty about having to tell Momma what was going on with Bree.

My stomach was in knots by the time I made it home.

"I'm back," I said nervously after I entered the house. Momma and Daddy were sitting in the living room, and Momma looked like she had been crying. "Is everything okay?"

Daddy looked up at me, and he looked the way I felt when I saw the result of Bree's pregnancy test: shocked.

I glanced at the living room table and my heart froze when I saw the pregnancy test sitting there.

I opened my mouth to speak, but Daddy noticed my gaze and stopped me. "I guess you know," he said, giving me this weird grin.

I nodded, not really sure what to say.

Momma started crying harder, and Daddy wrapped his arms around her, murmuring something about everything being okay.

"How could this happen?" she asked, looking at me for an explanation.

That's when it hit me that they thought the test was mine.

"I'm not pregnant," I said.

Momma and Daddy looked at me in confusion. "Who said anything about you being pregnant?" Momma asked through her tears.

It was my turn to look confused. "So you know?" I asked, assuming they'd found out about Bree.

"Know what?" Momma and Daddy looked at me

waiting for an explanation, but I didn't know what to say. If they didn't know Bree was pregnant, and I knew for a fact I wasn't, then that only left one option. My eyes widened as I felt myself about to throw up in my mouth.

My fear was confirmed when Cory bounded into the room all excited and exclaimed, "I'm going to be a big sister." She looked at me and grinned. "You're going to be a double big sister."

"You're pregnant?" I accused Momma.

She sat there blushing and nodding while Daddy got this huge grin on his face.

"You're pregnant." This time it was more a statement. My parents—who were pushing forty—were about to have a baby? I started getting sick all over again. "You can't be serious. What are my friends going to think?"

Saying the word *friends* made me think of Bree. I couldn't believe she and my mother were both having babies. The thought of it weirded me out so much I had to push it out of my mind.

"Am I going to have a brother or sister?" Cory asked.

Momma and Daddy laughed. "It's too early for us to know that," Momma said.

She stood, and I looked at her and realized she was huge, like she was at least about five or six months. How had I not noticed that?

"How far along are you?" I asked.

"I'm not sure, but I think a few weeks. I would say two months at most."

I looked at her skeptically. "Are you sure?" I didn't want to hurt her feelings, but before I could stop myself, I said, "Maybe you should find out for sure."

"I have a doctor's appointment tomorrow."

"What time?" Daddy asked.

"Ten," Momma said. "I need to go to the bathroom."

Daddy and I looked at each other as Momma walked out of the room, and I knew he knew that I wasn't happy.

"No matter what you're feeling, you need to support your mother. She needs us right now."

I nodded.

"Are you mad?" Cory asked.

I ignored her. "I'm going to my room." Suddenly I was tired. It was a long day, and I just wanted to crawl into bed.

Daddy nodded.

I met Momma as she was coming out of the bathroom, and she gave me a hug. "You might not see it now, but this baby is going to be a blessing."

"If you say so," I said.

I flopped across my bed, really just wanting someone to talk to. Before I realized it, I was calling Aidan, and I smiled when he answered.

"Hey, beautiful," he said.

"Hey," I said, knowing my sudden depression was all in my voice.

"What's wrong?" he asked.

I ignored his question. "You want to hang out?" I said. "I really want to see you."

"Sure," he said without a moment's hesitation. "I'll come get you."

"No, it's too far for you to come out here. Why don't we just meet at Bruster's in Vestavia?" I said, referring to the popular ice cream place.

"Are you sure you don't want me to come get you?"

"Boy, stop being silly. Can you be there in about thirty minutes?" I didn't know how I was going to talk Momma and Daddy into letting me go since they didn't like me going out at night by myself.

They must have still been focused on the baby, because after I lied and told them I was meeting Bree, they agreed.

I hopped in Momma's Pilot and zoomed to Bruster's, which was about fifteen minutes away, remembering to call Bree to tell her not to call me. When I got there, Aidan was just pulling up. He walked over to the car, smiling, and I couldn't help but smile, too, as he opened my door for me and helped me out of the car.

I threw myself into his arms, wanting him just to hold me, and he did.

"You want to talk about it?" he said when I finally let go.

I told him about not making the team and about Momma being pregnant, and he just listened. When I was done, without a word, he got up and returned a few minutes later with strawberry cheesecake ice cream, which happened to be my favorite, along with a cup of water, which I always had to have after eating ice cream.

I looked at him curiously, wondering how he knew.

He shrugged, looking a little embarrassed. "You told me one time it was your favorite."

"And you remembered that?" I asked. I didn't even remember saying it.

"I remember everything you tell me," he said.

I blushed and looked at the ground, but I knew he saw me smiling.

He plopped down next to me, and we sat in silence eating our ice cream and watching the cars zip past on Highway 31.

"So what are you going to do about not making the team?" he asked.

"There's really nothing I can do. I guess it just wasn't meant to be. I can still play this summer, so it's cool." As I said the words, I realized it was true. Just because the coach was an idiot didn't mean he would stand in the way of me playing basketball.

"You can always play me," he said.

"You mean beat you," I said.

"Oh, it's like that?" he said. "You think you can beat me in ball?"

"I know I can," I said, but really I wasn't so sure. I had seen Aidan play, and he was really good, better even than Allen.

"I'll have to take you up on that offer," he said.

I was about to invite him over to my house when I remembered Momma didn't want me dating him. "Just name the time and the place."

He nodded, shoveling a spoonful of what looked like every flavor of ice cream plus whipped cream, hot fudge, nuts and a cherry into his mouth.

"How can you eat all that?" I asked.

"It's good," he said. He spooned up some more and held it out to me. "Taste it."

I leaned forward and took a hesitant bite, allowing it to sit in my mouth for a second so I could sample all the flavors. "It's better than I thought it would be," I finally said.

He looked at me, and his eyes filled with laughter.

"What?" I asked.

"You have whipped cream on your face."

I swiped at my jaw, which only made him laugh harder. "You missed it."

"Well, why don't you get it for me?"

He reached for a napkin out of the dispenser that was sitting on our table, but instead of using it, he leaned forward and kissed the whipped cream off my cheek. As he pulled back, our eyes met, and suddenly our lips were moving toward each other, and the next thing I knew I was sharing the sweetest kiss I had ever experienced.

I was awakened early Sunday morning by my cell phone ringing. I thought about ignoring it, but I realized there were only one or two people who would call me at four in the morning, and if they did, it had to be important.

"Hello," I said sleepily.

"I've decided to get rid of it."

"What?" I sat up in bed, trying to clear the sleep fog from my brain. It took a split second for the words to register and for me to identify the caller.

"Bree?" I said.

"Yeah, it's me." Only, the voice sounded nothing like my best friend.

"Are you okay?" I said.

"I've decided to get rid of it," she repeated.

Her words really registered this time, and I snapped on my lamp, hoping maybe the light would change the truth of what Bree had said.

"Are you sure you want to do that?" I asked.

There was a long silence, and I wondered if maybe the call had dropped, but then I heard sniffling, and I realized Bree was crying.

"I can't have a baby," she said. "What am I going to do with a baby? I'm only seventeen."

I just sat there in silence. I knew Bree well enough to know she really didn't want an answer. More than anything, she needed someone to listen while she sorted things out.

"How can I tell my mom I'm pregnant? She will kill me."

"No, she won't," I said. "She might be mad, but she won't kill you."

"What would I do about college?"

I fell silent again, knowing she was once again trying to sort things out.

"Oh God," she cried. "I'll be a baby momma."

Despite ourselves, we both giggled.

"Seriously," she said a few seconds later. "I've decided to get rid of it. Will you go with me?"

As much as I didn't support what my best friend was doing, there was no way I could let her go through it alone. Over the years, Bree had shown herself to be a great friend—more like family really—and I knew I would always have her back.

"I'll be there," I said.

Thursday night, I told my mother I had a meeting after school the next day and thankfully she didn't ask a bunch of questions. Since she had confirmed she was three months pregnant at her doctor's visit, she was sleeping a lot and eating everything in sight. Daddy was waiting on her hand and foot, and lucky for me, they weren't being as strict as they normally were.

I was anxious the entire day at school, praying Bree would change her mind, but after the final bell, she was waiting beside Nathaniel's car, just like she said she would be.

"You sure you want to do this?" I asked.

She nodded, but I could see in her eyes she was scared.

"Bree, you don't have to do this," I said. "I'll help you take care of the baby, and I know Nathaniel will, too."

"But what if he doesn't?" she said, and her bottom lip started quivering.

"You know Nathaniel's not like that. I've known him all my life. He takes care of his responsibilities," I said.

It was true. I had known Nathaniel since kindergarten, and he had always been a nice guy. For a minute I'd had a crush on him, but that was back in elementary school. It had surprised me when he and Bree started dating, but the more I thought about it, the more it made sense. They had similar personalities, and they shared the same interests. I was happy they were together, and as far as I was concerned, Bree having a baby wasn't going to change that.

"What if he doesn't stick around? My mom thought my dad would, and he stayed long enough for me to be born. He told her he was going to make it big then he was going to come back for her, but he never did. What if Nathaniel does that to me?" A single tear fell down her cheek, and my heart broke for her.

I had never really thought about how hard it had to be for Bree not having her dad around. I had gone through a period for about two years where mine lived with us but he really wasn't there, and I knew how that had affected me. What would it have been like if he'd never been around? I guessed that really would have been hard.

"I have to do this," she said. "I can't depend on Nathaniel being there." She grew silent for a minute and sighed. "You know, during all those Worth the Wait meetings when Andrea was talking about saving yourself for marriage, I have to admit there was a part of me that didn't understand what the big deal was. I guess I figured if you and the guy loved each other and planned on being together anyway, why wait, you know?

"Now I'm starting to get it. Last night it occurred to me that if everyone waited until they got married to have sex for the first time and only slept with their spouse, we wouldn't have any sexually transmitted diseases."

I thought about what she was saying, and I realized she was right. Waiting until you got married to have sex for the first time would change a lot of things for a lot of people, but the truth was there didn't seem to be a whole lot of people who were waiting.

"I can't believe I was so stupid," Bree said. "I love Nathaniel, but—"

"But what?" Nathaniel asked, surprising us both.

"But I'm scared you'll leave me," Bree admitted honestly.

"I'm scared, too," Nathaniel said. I don't think I had ever seen him look so terrified. "I promise that we're going to get through this together. I told you I want you to have the baby, but I'm going to be there no matter what you decide to do, okay?"

He walked over and wrapped Bree in his arms, and I felt like I was peeking in on this moment, just like the time I saw Aunt Dani telling Miles she was pregnant. A few hours later, Allen had hit Aunt Dani with his car and left her for dead. I didn't have any doubt that Nathaniel wasn't planning on going anywhere.

"We can make this right right now, baby," he said. I watched in shock as he got down on one knee there in the parking lot and pulled out a ring bigger than the one Miles had been planning to buy for Aunt Dani. Bree and I both gasped.

"What are you doing?" she asked.

"Sabrina Davis, I love you, and I've told you before I want to spend my life with you. Will you do me the honor of being my wife?"

Bree looked at him with tears streaming down her face, and I saw the love shining in her eyes, but there was doubt, too. "You're just doing this for the baby," she said.

"No," he said, shaking his head so hard I thought it was going to come off. "I'm doing it because I love you. Bree, I want to be with you. Come on, baby, we've talked about this. We know we want to be together, so why can't we do it now?" He pushed the ring toward her, and she looked at it then looked at him then looked at me.

I couldn't explain it, but Nathaniel proposing felt right. I really believed he loved Bree with all his heart and that he would never do anything to hurt her. I suddenly wanted this for Bree as much as Nathaniel wanted it for them. I stared at the ring, wanting Bree to make a decision on her own, and I realized it was one that had been in Nathaniel's family for years. He had shown it to me a long time ago. His grandfather had given it to his grandmother, and after she had died when we were in sixth grade, Nathaniel told me it had been given to him to one day give to his wife.

It really was a beautiful ring, not like one of those

clusters that women used to wear back in the day. It was about two carats in a gold band in some cut I had never seen before.

"What if I decide not to have the baby?" Bree asked. "Will you still want to marry me?"

"Yes," Nathaniel said, almost before she could get the words out.

"Okay," she said.

"Okay what?" he asked, but he was already starting to grin, and so was I.

"Okay, I'll marry you," she said.

"What?" he asked, pretending he hadn't heard her.

"I said, okay, I'll marry you." She started laughing, and so did he, and she jumped into his arms.

I felt like I was back on the cheerleading squad I was grinning so hard, and if we weren't on the gravel, I would have done a back handspring.

Nathaniel took the ring from the case and placed it on Bree's ring finger, and I rushed over to check it out. She grinned at me and bounced in place, and, seriously, she looked as if she was glowing. I don't know if it was from the pregnancy or the excitement of Nathaniel proposing.

I only glanced at the ring for a second before wrapping her in a bear hug and Nathaniel joined us. We stood there for what seemed like hours, Nathaniel and I both surrounding Bree, letting her know that everything was going to be all right and that whatever she decided we had her back.

ten

A few days after Nathaniel proposed to Bree, I found myself presiding over a Worth the Wait meeting. Although my body was there, my mind and heart really weren't into what I was doing, and I guess it showed, because someone finally called me out.

"What's got you out of it today?" Felicity asked.

I shrugged, not sure I could really explain it myself. The last few days had been kind of bizarre. Bree still hadn't decided for sure what she was going to do about the baby, and my momma had dropped a bombshell that was ten times worse than her being pregnant: she was expecting twins.

She and Daddy had been grinning when they told me the news. I thought it was ridiculous. They were too old to be having one baby. Now they were going to add two to the mix. My only relief was that I would be going off to college soon, so I hoped I would miss a lot of the midnight feedings. I was assuming Bree wasn't going to keep the baby and we were going to go off to school and room together like we had always planned.

I hadn't realized until about thirty minutes before our meeting that that wasn't going to happen because this time next year Bree was going to be married.

"Hello," Jennifer said, waving her hands in front of my face. "Do you want to talk? Obviously you have some serious stuff on your mind."

"I'm okay," I said, then I just kind of stared off in space.

Finally, Jennifer pushed me aside and took charge of the meeting, and I smiled my thanks. I had done a lot of research about purity conferences and the ball, and she was easily able to follow my notes and toss out several ideas for things we could do after the committees reported. Once everyone started brainstorming, we came up with some more really cool ideas. We decided girls between the ages of ten and eighteen would be able to participate in the ball, and the conference was open to anyone who paid, although we were going to target high-school and college students. We even decided to set up MySpace and Facebook accounts to help publicize the event.

"I'm still not feeling this, y'all," said Briana Nunez. She had only recently joined, and she reminded me of a Hispanic version of my old cheerleading teammate, Rene White—she always had something negative to say. "It's going to look like we're marrying our daddies."

"No, it's not," someone else argued. "I look at it like he's giving me away. That's what I want my dad to do when I get married, so what's the big deal?"

Briana shrugged. "I don't know if I'm going to participate, and what about the girls who don't have fathers to escort them?"

Her words made me think of Bree, who didn't have a father to escort her, that's if she decided not to have the baby and came back to Worth the Wait. I had just kind of assumed everyone knew their fathers, but maybe I was wrong.

"They can ask an uncle or somebody," Jennifer said. "If we have that situation, we'll figure something out. We're not going to keep somebody from taking the pledge if they really want to."

We wrapped up the meeting, and as we were heading out, Nadia walked in.

I glanced at my watch then looked at her, silently questioning why she was just showing up when I'd told her the meeting was supposed to start at six-thirty.

She smiled an apology as she walked over to me. "I'm sorry I'm late. I was working on a difficult piece for my Juilliard audition, and I lost track of time."

"It's okay," I said. "Are you going to join?"

"I really just wanted to check out a meeting before I make a decision. When do you meet again?"

I explained we met every other week, and she frowned then explained she would be practicing for the next few months during the time we were holding meetings. "I don't know why it didn't click that your meetings would always be at the same time," she said.

"Girl, handle your business. We'll be here if you ever decide to join," I said as I packed up my stuff to leave.

There were only a few girls still hanging around, so I introduced her to them and our adviser, Andrea, before I gave Andrea a hug and Nadia and I headed outside.

"Where are you thinking about going to school?" she asked.

I stopped struggling with my keys and looked at her blankly for a second before it occurred to me she meant college, not high school.

"I'm thinking about the University of Alabama, University of North Alabama and maybe somewhere in Atlanta," I said. "I really haven't settled on any place. I don't even know what I want to major in yet."

"You should get started on your applications soon," she said. "A few of my friends from my school in Atlanta have known where they've wanted to go since they were in elementary school. They've already applied and are waiting for an early decision."

"What's that?" I asked, wrinkling my nose.

"It's where you apply to a school before the actual deadline with the understanding if they accept you you'll go there."

"Oh," I said, nodding in understanding, although part of me really didn't. "What happens if you have two schools you really like?"

"Then you should just apply to both schools for regular admission so if you get into both of them, you'll get to chose where you go."

That made me feel a little better. I still wasn't sure where I wanted to go, and I didn't like the idea of being locked into one school.

"So how long have you been playing the piano?" I asked.

"Since I was four," she said. "Momma said I just sat down at the piano one day and started playing."

I had heard of musicians like Alicia Keys and Prince playing by ear, but I had never met anyone who could actually do it.

"So you can play anything?" I asked, really fascinated.

She nodded, then shrugged like it was no big deal.

"Do you write, too?"

"Yeah. How did you know?" she asked, looking really surprised.

"It just seems like you would. Can you play something for me sometime?"

"I don't know," she said, hesitating.

"What's the big deal? You want to play in front of millions of people someday, don't you? I know you're not nervous playing for one person."

"Yeah, but I know you. What if you don't like what I play?"

"What if I do?"

She thought about what I said and grinned. "I guess I never thought of it that way," she said. "Okay. I'll play for you."

"Cool. When can I come over?"

"Are you sure you're coming to see me play the piano, or is it really my brother you want to see?"

The thought had crossed my mind. "Well…" I said. We looked at each other and burst out laughing.

"Why don't you spend the night one weekend?"

I got a sudden image of Aidan seeing me in my pajamas or watching me while I brushed my teeth, then I thought about having to go to the bathroom at his house, and I knew there was no way I would spend the night.

"My momma trips about letting me spend the night if she doesn't know the parents," I said, knowing it sounded crazy. I was almost eighteen, and although I knew the excuse was coming in handy, deep down I knew Momma really would have something to say.

"Yeah, my mom is the same way," Nadia said. "And if your dad is anything like mine, he would really have something to say if he knew a boy lived in the house."

I nodded, understanding. Since all the stuff with Allen, Daddy had become pretty protective of me—of Momma and Cory, too. I tried to pretend I didn't like it, but really I did. It felt good to know my daddy was worried about me because for so long he'd acted like he wasn't.

"Yeah, my daddy can be kind of crazy when it comes to boys, too. When I met Allen last year, he wouldn't let us date for the longest time." I thought about how differently things would have been if I had never dated Allen. "I wish now he'd kept saying no."

"He probably wishes he had kept saying no, too,"

Nadia pointed out. "How are you doing with the whole Allen thing?"

"It's still hard," I admitted. "It makes it hard to trust a guy, although Aidan is making things much easier." I quickly added the last part, remembering a moment too late that I was talking to his sister.

"You know you can talk to me, right? I would never tell my brother about anything we discuss."

"I know you wouldn't," I said, and really meant it. "I like your brother—a lot."

"Yeah. He's a good guy. He was asking about coming to the meeting, but I told him I thought it would only be girls here. I promised I would check it out first and let him know."

"Do you really think he'll come, even if he's the only guy?"

"Aidan doesn't care about that. He really believes in being a virgin until he's married, and he doesn't care who knows that."

"I think that's so cool," I said. "When I first joined Worth the Wait, I didn't want everybody to know, but the more I thought about it, I realized being celibate was a very big deal."

"So you're celibate?" she asked.

No one had ever come so close to asking me outright if I was a virgin. "I'm a virgin," I said proudly, "but I said *celibate* because a lot of girls in the club have had sex before and they decided not to again until they get married."

"I bet that's hard," she said.

"A lot of them say it is," I said, "but they are determined no matter what that they are worth the wait. They've decided not to let anybody or anything get them to break the promise they've made to themselves."

"I'm going to keep my promise, too," she said.

Something about her words made me wonder if she was a virgin, but before I could ask, my cell phone blasted "A Song for Momma," by Boyz II Men, and I grinned at Nadia, a little embarrassed as I answered the phone.

"Where are you?" Momma asked before I barely got the word *hello* out of my mouth.

"Still at church," I said.

"Your meeting ended thirty minutes ago," she said.

I glanced at my watch, realizing it had been thirty minutes, not believing she was making a big deal of it. "I lost track of time," I said. "I was talking to one of our new Worth the Wait members." Nadia and I smiled at each other. "I'm leaving right now," I said.

"On the way home, can you stop and get me some butter pecan ice cream, some ranch dressing and an order of beef with broccoli with extra hot sauce from Good Friends?" she asked, referring to the Chinese food place not too far from our house.

"Okay," I said slowly, wondering if she was planning on eating all that at one meal.

"You have money, right?"

"Yeah, I still have the emergency twenty you gave me."

"Use it," Momma said. "This is definitely an emergency."

"You're going to eat all that together?" I asked.

"Yes," she snapped. "Hurry up. I couldn't get in touch with your daddy, and I'm starving."

"I'm leaving right now," I said and hung up.

Nadia and I gathered our things, and we walked out together.

"I know you might not be able to make the meetings," I said, "but I really hope you'll join." A great idea struck me as we reached my car. "You can play for our purity ball."

She looked a little surprised. "Don't you need to run that by your club members?"

"They'll agree," I said, "especially if you're a member of the group. There are a couple of other girls who are members who can't attend meetings. This will be great. There are going to be a lot of people there, and there will be a lot of media coverage. Maybe you can write a song for us."

"Cool," Nadia said, warming to the idea. "What kind of song would you like?"

"Can we talk about it later?" I asked as Momma's ring tone blew up my phone again. "My momma's pregnant, and apparently the babies want some food." Nadia opened her mouth to speak, but I held up a finger, indicating she needed to wait a minute. "Hello," I said.

"Can you get an order of lemon-pepper wings, too?" Momma said.

"Yes, ma'am," I said as Nadia waved goodbye and held a pretend phone up to her ear to let me know she would call me later. I nodded as I got in Momma's car. "Anything else?"

"No, that should be good," Momma said.

The babies hadn't even arrived yet, and already they were driving me crazy.

Momma was sitting on the sofa propped up by pillows when I got home, and Cory was next to her rubbing her feet.

"Here you go," I said, placing the Chinese food on the table in front of her. I'd remembered I had an extra twenty Daddy had given me earlier in the week, so I had also stopped at McDonald's and gotten a Chicken McNugget Happy Meal for Cory and a manager's special—double cheeseburger, medium fries and medium Sprite—for me.

I had gone to McDonald's with Aunt Dani once, and she had frowned after taking a bite of her burger, making a big deal because they put ketchup and mustard on it. I didn't realize they made them differently in other parts of the country. I couldn't imagine eating them without mustard.

Cory went to wash her hands while I stood there watching in amazement as Momma pulled all the food I had for her out of the bags and started wolfing it down, only stopping long enough to ask for more hot sauce.

The amount of food she was eating was crazy. Even

Cory sat and stared when she came back downstairs. I finally had to leave the room when I saw Momma putting hot sauce on her ice cream. I headed to the den because I thought I was going to be sick to my stomach.

I took a few minutes to get myself together then attacked my food, laughing when I realized I probably looked just as bad as Momma. Afterward, I got comfortable on the sofa, wishing I had gotten a parfait, and flipped through the channels, stopping at an old rerun of *The Cosby Show* where the character Denise was telling her parents she wasn't going to college.

It made me think about my conversation with Nadia, and I realized I hadn't done a lot of research on schools. Although part of me knew I was supposed to graduate from high school in a few months and that soon I would be in college, it wasn't real yet. I had to make some decisions. I snapped off the television and headed over to the computer. After getting on the Internet, I sat staring blankly for a moment, not really sure how to go about searching. Finally, I typed in *Alabama colleges,* and a bunch of Web sites came up. I clicked on a few, but didn't stay on them long because I figured if the Web sites weren't cool then the school was not somewhere I wanted to be.

Somehow I ended up on the site for the University of Alabama at Birmingham. The Web site had a lot of good information, and although I'd told Cory differently, something about going to school in Birmingham appealed to me.

I was still on the site when Daddy walked in.

"Hey, baby," he said, dropping a kiss on my forehead.

"Hey, Daddy," I said, giving him a slight smile before I returned my focus to information about UAB's women's basketball team. Maybe I would be able to play college ball.

"So you're looking at schools," Daddy said.

I glanced at him. "Yeah. UAB looks pretty good."

"It's a good school," Daddy agreed. "I still hate I didn't graduate from there."

"Why didn't you?" I asked.

He gave a dry laugh. "Life," he said. "I was only about thirteen credits shy of graduating."

I looked up in surprise, never having heard that before. "Are you serious?"

"Yeah. Looking back on it now, I can't believe I was so close, but I was young then, and although my parents told me it was important to go to school, I didn't believe it. I had just found out I was adopted, and I didn't really want to hear anything they had to say. The night they told me about being adopted was when I took my first drink, and I think that was also probably the time I made the decision to not go back to school.

"My parents raised me right—I was in church every Sunday—but I felt like they had lied to me, and I didn't want to have anything to do with them or the things they had taught me. I dropped out of school, and I didn't speak to them for a few years. The next time I saw my mother was at my daddy's funeral."

He got choked up, and I felt sorry for him. As much as Momma and Daddy got my nerves, I couldn't imagine not speaking to them for years. Even as mad as Aunt Dani had made me by seeing Allen behind my back, I knew at some point we would be cool again. A man wasn't worth losing family.

Suddenly the whole conversation made me sort of depressed. "So where do you think I should go to school?" I asked, wanting to change the subject.

Daddy actually looked a little relieved. "I've always seen you as a Bama girl," he said. "I think the University of Alabama at Tuscaloosa would be good for you."

"Really?" I asked, sounding a little hurt. "You don't want me to stay home?"

He laughed. "It's not about what I want," he said. "If it were up to me, you would never leave home. I think it will be good for you to experience life on your own. I remember when my friends went off to school…. They all seemed to have a different experience from what I had still staying at home. I always said if I had kids, I would encourage them to go off to school."

"You knew when you were in college you wanted kids?" I asked.

"Actually, I made the decision after I found out I was adopted. For a while I found myself searching for my real family." He stopped and looked as though he was thinking about what he'd said. "Not that I didn't have a real family, but I wanted to meet the woman who gave birth to me."

"Did you ever think about looking for her?"

"I looked for her. I found a letter from her after my parents died, and I went to Columbus, Georgia, where she was from, and I found out she had died the same week."

"Wow. I'm sorry, Daddy." I knew it sounded lame, but I didn't know what else to say.

"I am, too," he said.

"Did she have more kids?"

"I don't think so," he said. "I was so shocked to learn she had died, I didn't ask."

"Who told you?"

"Some old relative of hers. She's gone now, too."

We sat in silence for a few minutes. "Why didn't you marry Momma a long time ago?" I had asked Momma that question months ago, but I really wanted to know how Daddy felt.

"Truthfully, I was too scared. I fell in love with your mother the first time I saw her. As the Commodores used to say back in the day, she was a brick house. I knew when I saw her on campus I wanted to spend my life with her." Daddy got this goofy look on his face, and although normally it would make me sick, this time it made me smile.

"Did she like you, too?"

He laughed so hard I thought he was going to hurt himself. "She couldn't stand me. She thought I was conceited, and she said every time she saw me I was with a different woman. Your mother was very focused, very driven. You remind me a lot of her. The older you get, the more you look like her, too," he said.

"So how did you end up together?"

"We were taking a class together, and I pretended I needed her help to pass it."

That reminded me of what Allen had done. What I was thinking must have shown on my face because Daddy said, "It was nothing like what happened with Allen. I still fault myself for what he did to you. Game should recognize game."

I couldn't help but laugh at the outdated phrase.

"Seriously," he said, "I knew what Allen was about the first day he walked into our house, but I let your mother and your aunt talk me into going against my gut. I'm a cop. It's my job to protect people, and I didn't even protect my own daughter. I'm sorry for that, baby. I promise you that will never happen again. The last thing I would ever want to do is hurt you, your mother or your sister—or the new babies."

His words made me feel good. I had missed having Daddy around after he had started drinking, but now that he had stopped, it was nice to have him back. When I was little, he never made a promise to me he didn't keep, and I knew this time would be no different. If he said he would never hurt us, then he wouldn't.

eleven

I met up with Aidan the next morning at school, and I couldn't help but smile as I looked at him.

He smiled back, which made him look even sexier, then leaned over to give me a big hug.

"Good morning, Courtland," he said.

Something about his words made me blush. "Good morning."

He smelled like he had just showered.

"We had to practice this morning," he said, as though he was reading my mind.

"Do you have practice later?" Suddenly I wanted to spend time with him. I had to sneak to talk to him at home since I wasn't supposed to, and now that basketball season had started, I really didn't see him after school.

"Yeah," he said, sounding tired. "Maybe I should skip it. Coach Patterson is really working us."

"You can't do that," I said. "Isn't a recruiter from the University of Alabama coming to the next game?"

"You're right," he said. "I guess I'm just having a bad day."

"Anything you want to talk about?" I asked. Aidan was so laid-back that I knew it had to be something pretty serious for him to be even the slightest bit upset.

"Not really," he said.

"You sure?"

He hesitated, and I could tell he was trying to decide whether to tell me. "Allen's friends were just doing a bunch of talk."

He didn't say it, but I knew it was about me. "What did they say?" I asked.

He hesitated again.

"Look, I want us to be honest with each other. I've had enough of guys not being honest with me."

"I know you're not trying to compare me to Allen," he said, looking annoyed.

"No. I'm just saying, if our relationship is going to work, we have to be honest with each other, even if it hurts."

He sighed. "You're right. There's a rumor going around that you're pregnant—by Allen."

"What?" I exclaimed. I don't know what I was expecting him to say, but it definitely wasn't that.

"They say you went to have an abortion last week and begged Allen to marry you so you could keep the baby."

I shook my head, not believing how gossip spread.

"Do you believe what they're saying?" I asked softly.

"Of course not. I know your virginity is just as important to you as mine is to me. I almost got into another fight again defending you."

"Please tell me you didn't," I said.

He shook his head. "A couple of my teammates grabbed me."

I didn't realize I had been holding my breath until he answered me. If he had gotten into another fight, he might have been expelled. I didn't think the school board would care if he was a star basketball player. They didn't play about fighting, and I didn't want Aidan to be labeled a troublemaker, especially since the only reason he was fighting was to defend me.

I gave him a hug. "Thanks for protecting me, but please don't get yourself in trouble. I don't want you to mess up your chance of getting a scholarship next year."

"I'm not going to let anyone talk bad about you," he said. "My dad raised me to believe you always protect the woman you love."

He said a few more things after that, but I was stuck on the love part. "You love me," I finally managed to say.

"Oh, you heard that part, huh? I was hoping I was talking so fast you would miss it."

"No, I heard you," I said.

"Courtland, I know we haven't been dating that long, but I really like you. I think about you all the time, and we're alike in a lot of ways. Maybe I do love you. I don't know because I've never been in love before."

I opened my mouth to tell him I loved him, too, but I stopped myself because I wasn't sure if I did. I knew I really liked him, and he was right, we were alike in a lot of ways. I had thought I loved Allen, but look where that had gotten me.

"You don't have to say you love me," Aidan said, although he did look a little hurt that I hadn't said the words.

"Aidan, I really care about you. I believe I love you, but I want to take things slow. I don't want to feel like I have to say it just because you said it first. I'm sorry if that hurts your feelings, but I have to be honest with you."

"I want you always to be honest with me," he said. "I don't want you to say anything you don't feel. I think taking things slow is a good idea. I plan on being around for a while."

"So do I," I said.

We were sitting in English class one day when two police officers appeared in the doorway along with Principal Abernathy.

I briefly wondered if something had happened to my dad, but my fears were erased when Principal Abernathy called out Allen. The class grew really quiet as Allen walked to the front of the room and gave the officers a charming smile.

"Is there a problem, Officers?" he asked.

One of the officers pulled out a set of handcuffs. "Allen Benson, you are under arrest for rape...."

"Man, what are you talking about? I didn't rape that

girl. She thinks because her daddy is the mayor of Mayfield, she can accuse me of something I didn't do."

I wondered if everyone else in the room was thinking the same thing I was, that Allen had told on himself. No one had said who he had raped.

An officer reached out to put the cuffs on Allen and started reading him his rights. Although my dad was a cop, I had never seen it done before, and I sat fascinated, secretly glad Allen was finally getting what he deserved.

My satisfaction didn't last long.

Before the officers could stop him, Allen bolted, and the officers and Principal Abernathy took off after him. The kids in my class ran to the door, but a few other teachers who had heard the commotion blocked us from leaving.

That didn't stop everyone from talking, though. Allen was the topic of the day, and I saw a lot of kids looking at me differently, like they were wondering if maybe I was telling the truth after all.

When I got home that afternoon, Allen was all over the news. He still hadn't been caught.

The next couple of weeks kind of flew by. Allen hadn't returned to school, and he still hadn't been arrested. There was a rumor he was in North Carolina with some relatives. His disappearance was good for me because I hadn't had problems from any of Allen's friends. Not having to worry about Allen gave me time to focus on other things. I had been thinking more and more about where I wanted to go to college lately, and after talking it over with Momma and Daddy, we decided to take a trip to visit the campus of the University of Alabama at Tuscaloosa.

Although it was only an hour away, I had never been there before, and as we approached the campus, I found myself getting excited. The campus was packed because there was some big game, and everywhere I looked there was something going on. We pulled up just as someone was leaving the administration building parking lot and slid right into their spot.

I couldn't believe how big the campus was.

"So, what do you think?" Daddy asked, looking around. I knew he was an Alabama fan, but he had promised he was going to let me make my own decision.

"It seems okay," I said, deciding it was best not to show my excitement. Suddenly I realized all I could do if I went off to school: I'd be able to stay out as late as I wanted attending parties and just hanging out with my friends, I didn't have to go to class if I didn't want to.... What was I ever thinking wanting to stay closer to home?

"Let's walk around," Daddy said. He grabbed Cory's hand and they were preparing to head off when I looked over at Momma. I could tell she didn't really like the idea. She had been having a lot of morning sickness, and I had overheard Daddy telling her to stay home, but she had said she'd be fine.

"What about if we just drive around?" I said. The

campus didn't seem to end, and I knew Momma wouldn't be able to cross the street, let alone the quad, which was a big grassy area on campus where students hung out.

Momma smiled her thanks, and Daddy looked at her and quickly agreed. We piled in the car and joined the long line of traffic with people trying to make their way to Coleman Coliseum. There seemed to be a good mix of people—blacks, whites, Asians and Hispanics. The fraternities and sororities were out in full force, sporting their Greek colors and letters. They all looked like they were having so much fun, and I couldn't wait to be a part of it.

I realized college was going to be a whole new world, and although I was excited about it, part of me was sad, especially when I realized Bree wouldn't be there with me. By the time I got ready to go away to college in the fall, Bree would be married with a baby. She had made the decision to keep the baby right after Nathaniel proposed.

I still couldn't believe it, and really Bree couldn't, either. We had talked about it a few times, and although she was excited about marrying Nathaniel because she really loved him, she was terrified about being a mom, especially without a college degree. Nathaniel was cool, but what if he tripped on her and left her to raise the baby alone? Bree's dad had done the same thing to her mom.

His name was Oz, and he had been in the rap game a long time. Although Bree had never met him, he did send her money every now and then. Bree's mom never spent it, though. It was sitting in an account somewhere to pay for Bree's college education.

That thought made me sad. Bree's mom had been working her whole life as a licensed practical nurse to give her daughter the college education she'd never had. Bree had been more upset about her mother's response to the pregnancy than about the fact she was actually having a baby. She said her mom had aged about twenty years right in front of her eyes. She was coming around, but I knew it still hurt Bree that she had hurt her mom.

"You getting nervous?" Momma asked.

"Huh?" I shook my head, trying to rid myself of the thoughts.

"Is all this overwhelming to you?"

"Kind of," I admitted. "I have a lot of decisions to make. I just want to make the right ones. I haven't made a lot of good ones lately."

"Yes, you have," Momma said. "Allen had us all fooled. You made one bad decision. Don't beat yourself up over it. Learn from it and move on."

"Okay," I said, suddenly feeling a little depressed.

Momma reached over and hugged me. "You're going to be fine," she said. "I'm really proud of you. I don't know if I could have handled things as well as you have."

"Thanks," I said.

Momma looked at me strangely. "What's wrong?"

I shrugged. "I was just thinking about Bree. We were

supposed to go off to college together." I had told Momma about Bree, and although she was disappointed, she was supportive.

"I know," she said. "A baby doesn't have to be the end of her life. Plenty of women have had babies at a young age and they've gone on to lead successful, fulfilling lives. Bree has a good head on her shoulders. She'll be fine. She'll find her way."

"I hope so," I said, praying deep down I would find mine.

By the time we got home, Bree was still on my mind, so I gave her a call, but she sounded sleepy, so I told her I'd talk to her later. I decided to call Aidan.

"How was the visit?" he asked.

"Good. I don't know if it's the school for me, though," I said. I guess I was still sounding a little down.

"Don't worry, you'll find the right school. You should check out UNA."

"Okay," I said, only half listening. My cheerleading cocaptain, Candy Harris, was at the University of North Alabama, and I heard from a few of the cheerleaders I was still cool with that she really liked it there.

"What's wrong with you?" he asked.

"Nothing," I said, not sure if I really wanted to talk to him about all that was going on in my head.

"You know you can talk to me about anything, right?" he said.

I took a deep breath, realizing he was right. Aidan had always been easy to talk to, and he was a really good listener. "I guess I'm just a little down because life is about to change so much," I said.

"But that's a good thing, right?"

"If you say so. It's just..." I took a deep breath.

"What?" he said, encouraging me to finish.

"I wasn't expecting to have to go through college alone, you know. Bree and I always talked about going to college together. It's not going to be the same."

"Maybe she'll still go," he said.

"Maybe," I agreed, but I really didn't believe it. It was easy for Bree to make plans before the baby came, but I was pretty sure babies required a lot of work. I was pretty young when Cory was born, but I remembered my mom being too tired to play with me or read to me.

"I can apply to the same schools you do," he said. "That way we can go together, and you'll know me."

"You'd do that for me? It's your dream to go to Bama," I said, really touched.

"I'd do anything for you, Courtland," he said, and I heard the sincerity in his voice.

"I'd do anything for you, too," I said. I could feel him grinning through the phone, and I knew it was as wide as mine.

"Maybe we can convince Nadia to apply with us," he said, and we both burst out laughing.

"Applying will be the only thing she's doing. You know she's going to Juilliard."

"I know," he said, sounding as sad as I had a few minutes earlier. "I'm going to miss her."

"Will it be the first time you've ever been separated?" I asked.

"We've gone to different camps and stuff a couple of times, but that was only for a week or two."

"So you understand what I'm feeling about Bree?" I said. "We've been together ever since freshman year."

"Yeah, I understand, but we're both going to be fine."

"So where do you want to go to college if you don't get into Bama?" I asked.

"I'm definitely thinking about UNA, but I'm also going to apply to Morehouse and Berkeley."

"You'd really go all the way to California for college? You'd never see your family."

"It's where my dad went, so I know he wants me to go there. We'll see. I'm not really sold on being that far away. At least if I went to Morehouse I'd be in Atlanta near my grandparents, and it's only a couple of hours from Birmingham, so I could come home pretty often. My dad's planning on going into business with my mom next year, so he'll be home."

"Are you guys close?" I asked. I suspected they were, but I had never asked.

"Yeah. Besides Nadia he's my best friend. He's the one who has kept me grounded with this whole basketball thing. For as long as I can remember he's always stressed to me and Nadia the importance of family."

"My dad and I just got cool again last year," I revealed.

"Really? Why?"

I explained how the summer before my freshman year, Daddy had been called to a bank robbery where a pregnant woman was being held hostage. The woman hadn't been married long when her mother died suddenly, and she and her husband had taken in her teenage sister. Daddy had promised the woman she would be okay, but the bank robber had killed her when his demands weren't met. Her husband had been so filled with grief he'd placed her sister in foster care. Daddy told me he felt like three lives had been lost that day, and although death was part of his job, I don't know if it had ever hit him that close to home before.

"I'm sorry to hear that," he said.

"He's doing much better now. Every time I turn around he's at an AA meeting. I'm really proud of him," I said, realizing it was true.

"I'm sure he's proud of you, too."

"I hope so. I've made some pretty messed-up decisions in the last year."

"What are you trying to say?" he joked.

"Boy, you know I'm not talking about you." I hesitated, wondering if I should talk about my old boyfriend to my new one. "Allen had my whole family fooled."

"I can see how that would happen." He took a deep breath. "I need to tell you something," he said slowly.

"What?" I asked curiously.

"I saw Allen the other day."

"Are you serious?" I said, my eyes growing huge. "Where?"

"My dad and I had gone to the mall, and he was there. I tried to ignore him, but he came over and spoke, but he couldn't take his eyes off my dad. It was like he had seen a ghost or something. The whole thing was weird. You know we can't stand each other."

"That is weird." I wanted to get more details, but I didn't want Aidan to think I was interested in getting back with Allen. I grew quiet, trying to figure out how to ask him, and Aidan started laughing.

"Go ahead and ask," he said.

"What are you talking about?" I said, trying to play dumb.

"You know you want the details of what we talked about."

"How do you know that?" I said.

"You forget I have two sisters," he said.

Aidan filled me in on the rest of the conversation, telling me Allen was bragging about beating the charges against him.

"So how are the plans for the purity conference coming?" he asked.

I knew he was trying to change the subject, so I played along. "They're coming along. I didn't expect the event to get so much attention, though."

"What do you mean?"

"We're the first group to sponsor one here in Birmingham, so Andrea has been getting a lot of calls from the media and people in other states who want to do conferences. I've even gotten some e-mails from kids, too.

Most of them like the idea, but there are a few who think the whole concept is kind of nasty."

"Nasty?" Aidan said, laughing. "Why do they feel like that?"

"Because we're making a pledge to our fathers and ourselves to remain virgins until we get married. A few of the e-mails I got said the idea of pledging that to their fathers weirded them out."

"Well, I think the whole idea is cool. Do you need an escort?"

It was my turn to laugh. "Boy, this isn't a debutante ball. My dad is going to escort me."

"Well, can I at least come?"

"You know you don't have to ask me that. Nadia is performing, so you have to support her," I said, but even as the words came out of my mouth, I wondered how my momma would react to seeing him there. She still didn't know we were together since she had broken up with him for me. I figured I had about five months to worry about that since the conference wasn't until April. I realized that didn't give us a lot of time.

"Let me let you go. I can hear you thinking over there," Aidan joked.

"You don't have to do that," I said as I reached for a notebook to jot down a few ideas.

"Bye, Courtland," he said, and I laughed.

"I'll see you at school tomorrow."

I talked to Andrea a few days later, and she agreed we needed to step things up with our planning for the purity conference. I suggested a slumber party so my Worth the Wait members and I could stay up all night if we needed to to get the details in order. Members weren't really feeling it at first, saying how a slumber party was for babies—until Andrea said she'd spring for a hotel room for the night, which got a lot of them excited.

I was worried that Momma wouldn't let me go since it was in a hotel, but she surprised me when she shrugged and said okay, adding that this time next year I would be in college so I needed to get used to sleeping away from home, which I had only done a few times, other than an occasional sleepover at my grandparents' or Aunt Dani's when she was in Birmingham.

I shook the thought of Aunt Dani from my mind. We hadn't heard from her since Momma and Daddy's wedding, and I didn't know whether that was good or bad. Although a part of me was still mad at her, deep down I realized she was my aunt, and I couldn't let a guy, especially someone like Allen, come between us.

The night of the slumber party, I packed up all my gear and headed to the Sheraton in downtown Birmingham. I had only been there once for our church scholarship banquet, and the place was huge, big enough for us kids to go in without being stopped and questioned by the staff. It was located right next door to the civic center, and apparently there was a Tyler Perry play in town that night, because the streets were packed. I had to drive around for ten minutes before I finally ended up parking a few blocks away near the Division of Youth Services and walking over.

Only three girls had already arrived when I got there, and I greeted them with hugs, once again remembering the lesson Andrea had taught me when she had hugged each of us during a meeting before revealing she was HIV positive.

"Where is everybody?" I said, throwing my sleeping bag, backpack and overnight bag on the floor.

"Jennifer just called me and said she was running late, and I guess everybody else is, too," Felicity said.

There was a knock on the door, and I went to answer it, frowning when I didn't recognize the two girls standing on the other side. "Can I help you?" I asked, figuring they had the wrong room.

"Is Felicity here?" one of them asked. She had a blond Mohawk, which didn't look right because she was very dark. She was the total opposite of the other girl, who was very light and sporting a short afro.

"Come on in, girl," Felicity said, running to the door.

"Who are they?" I asked.

"That's my cousin Angel," she said, pointing to the girl with the Mohawk, "and that's her friend Yasmin. I told them about Worth the Wait and they want to join. I figured they could come tonight to meet everyone."

Yasmin looked like she was trying to keep from laughing.

"I don't know…" I said slowly. "This is just supposed to be for people who are already active in the group.

Maybe we need to wait until Andrea comes and run this by her."

"Oh, I forgot to tell you, she won't be here tonight. She called and said she was with her fiancé in the emergency room. The doctors think he might have food poisoning."

I realized if what Felicity was saying was true, I wouldn't be able to call Andrea since phones weren't allowed in some parts of hospitals. I decided to call anyway, and the call went straight to voice mail. I didn't bother to leave a message.

Four more girls, including Briana and Jennifer, arrived, and we ordered pizza then got down to business, checking on the progress of each of the committees we'd set up. Most of them had done a lot of work, but I wasn't surprised to find Felicity, who had volunteered to do entertainment, hadn't done anything lately.

"So we don't have music or anything for the conference confirmed?" I asked, annoyed. Everyone knew entertainment was crucial, and most of the good entertainers were booked months in advance.

"I'll take care of it next week," Felicity said, shrugging.

"No, we're going to take care of it tonight. I knew we shouldn't have put you over entertainment," I muttered.

"Are you talking to me?" she asked.

I looked her dead in the eye, just like my daddy had taught me to do, trying to ignore the nerves doing backflips in my stomach. "Yes," I said. "I'm going to put someone else over entertainment."

"I'll do it," someone volunteered. "My cousin is friends with DJ Strick from 95.7 Jamz. I'll see if we can get him."

I nodded and wrote that down in my notebook.

"How you gon' just take a committee from her?" Felicity's cousin Angel asked. Despite my protests, the other members didn't have a problem with Angel and Yasmin being there.

"I'm the president. If she's not doing her job, then we'll find someone who will," I said, nodding at Tracy, who had volunteered for the position.

"She's just jealous of me," Felicity said.

"I don't even know you," I said.

"Guys, break it up," Jennifer said. "We're supposed to be working together and having a good time."

Felicity turned to me like Jennifer hadn't said a word. "You're just mad because I'm dating Allen now."

Her words surprised me, but I didn't let it show. "And?"

"Allen told me how you've been calling him trying to get back with him."

I gave a dry laugh. "Girl, please. You can have Allen. I wouldn't touch him with a ten-foot pole. If you had any sense, you'd stay away from him. He has about five girlfriends."

"I know he has other girls. I have other guys, so what's the problem?" she said, raising up at me like she was going to do something. "You trying to call me stupid?"

I ignored my nerves again, trying to play it cool. "You said it, I didn't," I said, turning my back to her.

I felt a gush of wind and turned around just in time to see someone grab Felicity to keep her from jumping on me.

"Girl, chill," Yasmin said. "You don't want to go back to juvie."

I raised my eyebrows and looked across the room at Jennifer, whose shocked expression, I'm sure, mirrored mine. We watched in stunned silence as Angel walked over to the stocked refrigerator and proceeded to fix three drinks from the miniature bottles of liquor and soda. "Anybody else want one?" she asked, handing Felicity and Yasmin drinks.

"What are you doing?" Jennifer finally managed to say.

"I'm trying to get this party started. Y'all acting all stiff in here. You need to loosen up." She dipped her finger in her glass, stirred, then licked her finger before taking a huge gulp and gritting her teeth. "Man, I tell you, that will put hair on your chest," she said, and she, Felicity and Yasmin laughed.

"Y'all have to go," I said. "We didn't come here to drink. We're supposed to be planning this purity conference."

"I bet your daddy wasn't thinking about purity when he was here the other night," Felicity said and started laughing.

I swung around, angry that she would let my daddy's name come out of her mouth.

"Felicity, that's not cool," Tracy said before I could respond.

"I said the same thing when I realized that wasn't your mother he was with." Felicity and Angel slapped hands then bent over and laughed so hard tears were streaming down their faces. "He tried to pretend he didn't know me when I spoke, but I'd know your fine daddy anywhere."

"Why would you say something like that?" Jennifer asked. She was so angry it was like Felicity was talking about her father.

"I'm just telling the truth."

"Y'all need to leave," I said quietly. I hadn't been so angry in a long time. I felt the pulse quicken in my temple, and I knew I was about to lose it.

"Ooh, look, she's mad," Angel said, pretending to shake like she was scared.

"For real, y'all need to leave," Jennifer said.

Felicity ignored her as she picked up her phone and glanced at what I assumed was a text. "The guys are on their way," she said.

"Guys?" I said. "What guys?"

"You didn't think we were going to stay out all night at a hotel and not invite some guys. There's no way I could pass up this *opportunity*." Her words were running together.

Jennifer and I looked at each other, not sure what to do when there was a knock on the door. I think we both had been hoping this was all a joke, but the joke was on us when two guys walked through the door, wearing pants that were sagging all the way to their ankles, white tank tops underneath Sean John jackets, iced-out grills and baseball caps.

They cranked up the music, and before I realized what was happening, a few of the other Worth the Wait members had called their best friends and boyfriends, and suddenly before I knew it, what was supposed to be a peaceful sleepover had turned into the party of the year. When Allen walked through the door, that was my cue to leave. Jennifer saw me grab my stuff and went to get hers, and we walked out the door, not looking back.

"Felicity is crazy," Jennifer said as we piled into my car. It was around midnight, and I knew Momma would have a fit about me being out so late, but I figured under the circumstances she would understand. I smiled, realizing a few months ago I probably would have been too scared to say anything and would have just locked myself in the bathroom until the party was over.

"Are you going to tell your parents?" Jennifer asked.

"Probably," I said. "My momma's going to want to know why I'm out in the middle of the night. Besides, we didn't do anything wrong."

"That's true. I guess we need to call Andrea since the room is in her name. A few of those people looked a little wild. I hope they don't wreck the room." She didn't wait for me to respond as she pulled out her phone and called Andrea. "She didn't answer," she said. "I'll just text her."

I nodded, keeping my eyes on the road. I sat there replaying the night's events in my mind, wondering how things had gotten so out of control. I thought about what Felicity said about seeing my daddy with another woman, and as much as I tried to shake the thought from my mind, I couldn't. He had been working a lot lately, and a few times, Momma or I had tried to get in touch with him, and we couldn't. I shook my head, clearing the thought of my daddy with another woman from my mind. There was no way he could be creeping on my mom. Could he?

twelve

when I got home, Momma was still awake, but Daddy was nowhere to be found.

"Where's Daddy?" I asked, taking off my coat and hanging it in the closet before going to kiss Momma on the cheek. She was sitting with her legs propped on the sofa, flipping through television channels.

"He left to go to the store about an hour ago," she said, sounding worried.

"Did you try calling him?" I said.

"Yeah, but the phone is just going straight to voice mail."

"Maybe his battery is dead," I said.

"Maybe," she muttered. She looked at me, like it just occurred to her I shouldn't be home. "What are you doing here?"

I explained what happened at the hotel, leaving out the part about Felicity accusing Daddy of cheating.

"I don't like you driving around so late, but I'm glad

you left," she said, giving me a hug. "I'll call your daddy again and tell him to send one of the officers by to check out the room."

I nodded. "You want something to eat?" I asked.

"Do you mind?" she said.

I shook my head. "I'll take a tuna sandwich on whole wheat with extra mayonnaise, pickles and some nacho chips."

I knew she had to be joking, so I waited for her to start laughing. Instead she sat there licking her lips like she had just ordered one of everything on Red Lobster's menu. "You're serious?"

She rubbed her stomach. "I know it sounds horrible, but it's for the babies. I've been craving it off and on for the last few days."

I shook my head, wondering if Bree was experiencing the same thing. As I made two sandwiches for Momma, figuring she needed one for each baby, I called Bree on her cell phone.

"Hey, girl, I was just calling to check on you," I said.

It took me a second to realize Bree hadn't responded. "Bree?" I said.

When she sniffled, I put down the knife and focused on the phone. "What's wrong?"

"I'm—" she said, before dissolving into tears.

"Bree. Bree?" I screamed. Suddenly I was scared. "What's wrong?"

"Courtland," Momma yelled from the den, "is everything okay?"

I ignored her as I tried to get Bree to talk to me. "Bree, what's going on?"

"I'm bleeding."

I sucked in a breath, knowing that couldn't be good. "I'm on my way," I said.

I hung up the phone and rushed into the den where Momma was struggling to get up from the sofa. She took one look at me and worry filled her face. "What's wrong?"

"It's Bree," I said. "I've got to go."

Momma grabbed me as I sped past her. "Go? Go where?"

"Bree's bleeding. She needs me. I've got to go."

"Courtland, it's too late for you to be leaving this house."

Before I could stop myself, I was screaming and crying. "My friend needs me, Momma. I'm going. I'll be fine."

Momma sighed, realizing nothing she said was going to stop me. "At least calm down before you walk out of here."

I went to the kitchen to get a drink of water and realized I hadn't finished fixing Momma's food. As much as I wanted to leave everything where it was and rush out of the house, I knew Momma was right. I did need to calm down. By the time I was done with the sandwiches, Daddy was walking through the door, and Momma insisted he drive me to Bree's house.

I tried calling Bree again to let her know I was on the way, but there was no answer, so I called Nathaniel, who told me he was on the way to meet her at St. Vincent's

Hospital. I told Daddy, and he headed in that direction while I prayed like I had never prayed before.

My prayers were in vain.

Bree lost the baby the next morning.

I had known Nathaniel all my life, but I had never seen him so torn-up. He had Bree wrapped in his embrace, and he was rocking her and he kissed her over and over, telling her how much he loved her and that everything was going to be all right.

Bree was in shock. I think everybody was. We had all grown used to the idea of her having a baby, and although it wasn't ideal circumstances, no one wanted her to lose her.

Did I mention the baby was a girl?

I think the fact it was a girl hurt Bree even worse. During the times when we would talk about our future, she would always talk about having one child, a little girl she wanted to name Maya.

Bree had to stay in the hospital a couple of days because her blood pressure was high, and each time I went to see her, she looked lost. I could tell she was de-pressed, but I didn't know how to help her, so I just sat there, holding her hand, ready to listen if she needed me.

It wasn't until the day she was supposed to leave that she finally spoke.

"Well, I guess I can go to college now," she said sadly.

I nodded, not really sure how to respond.

"Have you decided where you're going to go?" she asked.

I knew she already knew the answer, but I played along. "Not yet," I said. "I didn't realize picking a school would be so hard."

"You figured out your major yet?"

Unlike me, Bree was sure she wanted to major in journalism. I couldn't seem to settle on what I wanted to do with my life. When I was little I used to say I wanted to be a doctor, but then I realized the sight of blood made me sick to my stomach, so that was out. I had even thought about journalism like Bree, and although I wasn't opposed to writing, I wasn't sure I wanted to spend my life doing it. I figured I would make a decision soon enough.

"How are the plans coming with the purity conference?" she asked. Before I could respond, she said, "I forgot to tell you I saw Emily in Wal-Mart pushing a baby stroller. She was with some Hispanic dude, and guess what she called him?"

"Allen," I said.

"Yup."

I just shook my head and laughed. Emily had been dating someone else named Allen all along. "Did she have a boy or a girl?"

"I don't know. My momma was rushing me, and Emily just waved and kept going. Finish telling me about the purity conference plans."

"We got everything worked out. Girl, I forgot to tell you what happened with Felicity the night we stayed in the hotel."

"What?" Bree said, leaning forward in the bed. For the first time in a while she looked like the old Bree, and I smiled.

I told her what had happened, and she just sat there shaking her head. "She gets on my nerves. I can't believe she's dating Allen and that she thinks you still want him." Bree looked at me curiously. "You don't still want him, do you?"

"No," I said, realizing I really meant it. When the school year had first started, I had tried to pretend I didn't still care about Allen, though deep down, I still did, but at some point that had changed. I realized if I never saw Allen again in my life, I would be cool. I couldn't help but smile at the revelation. For the first time in a while, I felt like I was taking a serious step toward learning to love myself. I couldn't help the goofy grin that spread across my face.

"What are you smiling at?" Bree asked.

"I was just thinking that I'm finally over Allen," I said.

Bree clapped. "It's about time. I never thought he was good enough for you."

"You didn't?" I said, surprised. "Why didn't you tell me?"

"I tried, but you were in so deep you weren't trying to hear anything I had to say." She shrugged.

"I'm sorry," I said. "If I don't know anything else, I know you've got my back and that you want what's best for me." I looked at her. "So what do you think of Aidan?"

She shook her head, and I was worried for a minute until I saw the corner of her mouth twitch. I popped her on the arm and she burst out laughing.

"Girl, you had me for a minute."

"If I were you, I would never let Aidan go. He's a great guy. I think the two of you make a good couple."

"I do, too," I said. "I wish my mom felt the same way."

"She'll come around," Bree said. "Have you tried talking to her again?"

"No. I already know what she's going to say."

"Maybe she'll surprise you."

"Maybe," I said, but I really didn't believe it.

"So what do you think of Nathaniel?"

Her question surprised me. "He's great," I said. "You know he's been my boy since kindergarten. You don't think so?"

Bree gave a sad smile. "He's wonderful," she said. "Do you think he's still going to want to be with me now?"

"Girl, you're being silly. You know Nathaniel is crazy about you. You losing the baby isn't going to change that." I bit my lips, trying to call back the mention of the baby. "I'm sorry."

"For what?" Bree said. "I did lose the baby. I just hope I don't lose Nathaniel, too."

She didn't look so sure. "Nathaniel loves you," I said. "I've never been surer of anything in my life."

"I hope so," she said. She reminded me of Cory, who

had come and asked to sleep in my bed one night after a bad thunderstorm. Just like I had done with my sister, I wrapped Bree in my arms and rocked her, letting her know that everything was going to be okay.

In all the years I had known Bree, she had always had my back, but this was the first time I truly felt like I had hers. It felt good to be there for my best friend to lean on. I promised myself right then and there, whenever Bree needed me, I was always going to be there, no matter what.

"Promise me we'll always be friends," I said.

Bree laughed and stuck out her pinkie finger, and I immediately wrapped mine around hers, like we used to do freshman year. "Girls for life," she said.

"Girls for life," I agreed.

The day Bree was released from the hospital, I met her mother and Nathaniel at the hospital. I couldn't believe all the flowers and stuff she had gotten. A few kids from school had heard what happened, and they had come to visit and sent cards, which really helped raise Bree's spirits. It also didn't hurt that Nathaniel had come to see her and told her he still wanted to get married.

Bree had agreed to stay engaged, but she really wanted to finish school before they got married, and I couldn't blame her. Nathaniel, as usual, was supportive. He just wanted to do whatever made Bree happy.

I helped get Bree settled at home, then I rushed out the door, realizing I was going to be late for our first purity ball practice. It really was going to be an elaborate event, and now that it was getting closer, I found myself more and more excited.

"Where are you running off to?" Bree asked.

"Practice," I said. "I'm meeting my dad there."

"Is it too late for me to sign up for the ball?" she asked.

I shook my head, a little surprised she would want to.

"Don't give me that look," she teased, and I laughed. "Seriously, I've been giving it some thought, and I want to get active again. Now I get why those girls who were pregnant still attended Worth the Wait meetings. It's kind of the same reason Andrea told us she was HIV positive. Not being a virgin shouldn't stop you from being active in the group. I think now I have more of an incentive to join. I want to make sure other kids don't mess up like I did."

She looked at Nathaniel apologetically, but he didn't seem offended at all. "Can I escort you?" he asked.

"Why do you guys keep thinking this is a debutante ball?" I said. "No, you cannot escort her. She needs an adult male role model to do it."

"Well, I can at least come, right?" Nathaniel said.

"You sound like Aidan," I said, then looked around, relieved when I realized Bree's mom wasn't in the room. The last thing I needed was for her to say something to my mom about Aidan. "This is not a debutante ball."

"Are you sure?" Nathaniel asked. "That's not what they were saying on the news last night."

"Maybe you were watching something about a debutante ball."

"No, I was watching something about your Worth the Wait chapter hosting a purity ball. It was on Fox 6."

"Are you serious?" I asked. I whipped out my phone, checking to see if someone had called or texted me to let me know our chapter was going to be on the news. I saw I had two missed calls and a few texts, which I quickly saw confirmed Nathaniel's story.

"What was the story saying?" I asked, making a mental note to go on Fox 6's Web site to see if I could watch the clip.

"They interviewed Andrea and I think someone named Jennifer. They were trying to explain why you were having the ball. Then they had these people on there protesting it."

"Protesting?" I said absently, wondering why Jennifer was being interviewed instead of me since I was president of the chapter.

"Yeah, people were saying what y'all are doing is weird."

I shook my head. "I heard someone else say that."

"Do you guys think it's weird?" I asked. I glanced at my watch, realizing I really needed to wrap things up or I was going to be late. I had been riding my daddy all week, reminding him to be on time, and the last thing I needed was to not be there when he showed up.

Bree shook her head. "I think it's great you have a man you trust enough to commit yourself to until you get married." Something told me she was thinking about her daddy.

"It is kind of weird," Nathaniel said. "I'm cool with taking the whole purity pledge, but why does your father have to be the one to escort you?"

"Because for most girls, their father is the first opportunity they have to see how relationships work." I had heard someone else say that, and it sounded good, but as the words were coming out of my mouth, I wondered if I really believed them. My daddy and I had had our ups and downs, and although we were in a good space now, what if things changed again?

"Girl, I know you're not going to stand here and argue with Nathaniel," Bree said. "You're going to be late."

I said my goodbyes and headed to practice, which was being held in the family life center of our church until the week of the actual event. Then we were going to the Harbert Center, the same place we'd had Momma and Daddy's wedding reception.

I got to the church about five minutes before we were supposed to get started, and I frowned when I searched the parking lot and didn't see my daddy's car. I sat in my car, figuring he would show up any minute, but when he still hadn't arrived ten minutes later, I headed inside where Andrea was busy explaining what we were going to be doing that night.

We all introduced ourselves, then each father and daughter got in line to begin learning the dance routine, which was being choreographed by a member of our church. Since I was the only one whose father wasn't present, I ended up being partners with Ms. Minnie, our choreographer. I don't know if I was more embarrassed to be dancing with her or that my daddy still hadn't shown up.

I thought about sending him a text, but I wasn't sure if he even knew how to receive one, let alone how to respond. Everyone was gathering their stuff when he finally showed up. I couldn't even look at him I was so angry. He tried to apologize, but he might as well have been talking Chinese because I wasn't hearing what he had to say. He knew how important the ball was to me, and for him to not show up said a lot.

I waited until I got in my car before I let the tears fall, wondering what was so important that he missed practice.

I remembered Felicity saying she had seen him with another woman. I thought back over the last few months and realized he hadn't been home a whole lot. He hadn't been drinking—or at least I didn't think he had—and he and Momma had both been complaining about not having a lot of money, so it didn't make sense he had been working all the overtime he claimed. The more I thought about it, the more I wondered if maybe Felicity was right.

Maybe Daddy was seeing another woman.

I got even more suspicious when he didn't come home until after midnight, even though I vaguely remembered him telling me he was right behind me. Momma was asleep, and I met him at the door, staring at him in disgust.

"Where have you been?" I asked, planting my hands on my hips.

He glanced at me and proceeded to hang up his jacket like I hadn't said a word, which made me even angrier.

"I know you heard me," I said, wondering where I was getting the strength to talk to my daddy that way.

"Courtland, please. I'm not in the mood," he said as he headed for the kitchen.

I followed him, quickly glancing upstairs to see if him walking in the door had awakened Momma. I was relieved when I saw their bedroom light was still off.

"Are you cheating on Momma?" I asked. He hesitated, and before he could speak, I continued. "That woman is up there pregnant with your twins, and you're cheating on her? You need to be ashamed of yourself." I looked at him in disgust. "After the way she has stood by you..." I couldn't even speak I was so angry. "I'm going to tell her," I finally managed, whirling around.

Daddy swung me back to face him, and I got scared. "I'm going to say this once, and I don't ever want to have this conversation again," he said in this deathly quiet voice. "I am not cheating on your mother. I never have cheated on her, and I never will."

"Then where have you been lately?" I asked. I was trying to pretend I was still in control, but deep down I was trembling. "One of my friends saw you with another woman." I ignored the fact that I was referring to Felicity as a friend when I knew she wasn't.

He laughed. "Your friend doesn't know what she's talking about."

I wanted to believe him, but something wasn't adding up.

"You better not hurt my mother," I said, determined to have the last word.

Things were pretty tense in our house for the next couple of weeks. Daddy showed up for practice, but I just went through the motions, secretly trying to figure out if there was someone else I could get to escort me.

On the day Momma was supposed to go have her ultrasound, Daddy was late showing up, and I looked at him in disgust as he gave Momma some tired excuse. I blocked him out, focusing instead on the images on the screen. At first it was pretty hard to figure out what I was seeing, then the sonographer switched to a 4D image, and my mouth dropped open. There, as clear as day, were the babies. One was sucking a thumb while the other threw up a hand as though he or she was waving at us. I looked over at Momma, and she was in tears. Cory and Daddy were just staring in amazement.

"Can we find out whether you're having boys or girls?" Cory asked.

Daddy looked like he really wanted to know, and I wondered if he was hoping it was a boy. I know when Momma had been pregnant with both Cory and me he had wanted a boy each time, and he had been really depressed when we turned out to be girls.

"I think I want to be surprised," Momma said.

"Baby, what's the harm?" Daddy said.

Momma looked like she was going to give in, but then I saw this look of determination come over her face. "No, we'll wait," she said.

I thought Daddy was going to protest again, but instead he shrugged and refocused on the screen.

"So I have to wait to find out what you're having?" Cory asked.

"I'm afraid so," Momma said. "It won't be much longer."

"I hope they are both girls," Cory said. "I can teach them how to play my Game Boy."

Momma and Daddy laughed.

"You'll have to wait a while on that," I said and gave her a hug after she frowned. "I'm going to remind you of how disappointed you are when you're complaining the babies are taking all your stuff."

"No, you won't," Cory said. "You'll be gone to college."

I hadn't really thought about that in a while. As much as I was looking forward to going off to school, it hadn't occurred to me that I would only be around for a month or two after the babies were born, then I'd be headed off to college. "I'll be home on weekends and holidays," I said.

"Promise?" Cory asked.

"Promise."

thirteen

I was sitting in math class when the long drone of the tornado-drill bell interrupted Mr. Mitchell's boring lecture. I groaned, not relishing the thought of having to sit in the hall with my head tucked between my knees. I filed out into the hall with the rest of my classmates, grinning when I spotted Aidan, Nadia and Bree, who had returned to school the day before.

"How long are we going to be out here?" I asked.

"Girl, hopefully not long," Bree said.

"You've had tornado drills before?" Nadia asked, sounding surprised.

I shrugged. "A couple of times a year. You never had them in Atlanta?"

"Not that I remember," she said. She looked at Aidan, who shook his head, confirming her words.

"I think they do it as more of a precaution than anything. I've never known for a tornado to actually hit in Birmingham," Bree said.

I thought about it. "Now that you mention it, I don't remember it, either," I said. "It's probably just another way for teachers to get out of teaching us."

We all laughed.

We ended up sitting in the hall for almost an hour and a half. My butt was so sore when I got up, I didn't think I would be able to walk for a week. Luckily, we didn't have to keep our heads down the whole time. It would have been a fun time if the citywide tornado alarm hadn't kicked in with its loud droning. That really had a few of the kids scared. I was cool until my homeroom teacher, Mrs. Ross, turned on her TV and all programming had been interrupted because there were reports of several tornadoes touching down around the city.

I thought about my family and wondered if they all were okay. I figured Cory was probably terrified because she didn't like bad weather, especially thunder and lightning.

I whispered a prayer that she and my parents were okay.

"You thinking about your family?" Aidan leaned over and whispered.

"Is it that obvious?" I asked.

He nodded then grabbed my hand and squeezed. "I'm sure they're fine. I was able to text my mom, and she told me she and my dad were at the shop and they were going to stay there until the storm passed. Nya's still in school."

"I didn't even think about texting them," I said, whipping my cell phone out of my purse. We weren't allowed to use them during school, but I saw quite a few kids and several teachers were using theirs, so I figured it wasn't a problem. "Your dad's in town?" I glanced at him quickly before refocusing on the message I was sending.

"Yeah, he's here for a couple days. He's already given notice, so he should be moved here by the time Nadia performs at the ball."

"I know you're happy about that," I said.

Aidan's eyes lit up. "Yeah, it will be good to have him around more. I miss him when he's gone."

"That's really sweet," I said.

"What?" he asked, totally clueless.

"I think it's great that you and your dad are so close, and that you don't have a problem saying so."

He shrugged. "When I care about people, I think it's important to let them know." He stared at me, and I blushed.

"I love you, Aidan," I said. I wasn't sure where the words came from, but I knew I meant them.

"I love you, too." He looked like he wanted to kiss me, but he looked over my shoulder, and whatever he saw made him change his mind. I glanced up to see Principal Abernathy headed toward us, messing up the moment.

"You guys okay?" he asked. He didn't even wait for us to respond before he spoke into the walkie-talkie he had in his hand.

I was just about to say something to him when my phone vibrated in my hand, letting me know I had a text. I breathed a sigh of relief when I saw it was from my mother. I quickly read it, and I couldn't help but laugh at her attempt at a text. I guess she was trying to be cool and use abbreviations, but not much of what she said made sense. The fact that she responded let me know she was okay.

I tried to text my dad, too, but thirty minutes later, I still hadn't gotten a response. I hoped he was busy working, but there was a part of me that wondered if maybe he was out with another woman. I pushed that thought out of my mind.

"Have you heard from your mom?" I turned and asked Bree. She had texted her mom and Nathaniel, who had a dentist's appointment that day.

"Nope," she said. "Knowing Momma, she doesn't even have her phone on, though."

I laughed. "Of all the parents in the world, why do we have the ones who refuse to come into the twenty-first century?"

"Girl, I don't know. I'm still surprised she actually let me get a cell phone."

"Have you heard from Nathaniel?"

She nodded. "He texted me to let me know he was home. He has to get his wisdom teeth pulled though."

I shuddered. "Better him than me. I heard that hurts."

We were in the hall another fifteen minutes before we got word we could go back to class. Since it was almost time to leave, Mrs. Watters didn't bother giving us an English assignment. Instead she kept her TV on, and we watched the breaking news on the tornado's damage.

The room fell silent. I don't think any of us had realized how bad it was outside until we saw the pictures. There were whole blocks wiped out in a few neighborhoods while in others the tornado had torn down one house and left the one next to it untouched. A few of the kids were freaking out when they saw their neighborhoods. I got scared and texted Momma and Daddy again, and I really got nervous when neither one of them had responded by the time we got out of school.

I called Momma the moment Bree and I got into the car. There wasn't an answer at home or on her cell. I went to pick up Cory, and she looked just like I had expected her to—scared out of her mind.

"Hey, munchkin," I said. "How was school?"

"We had a tornado drill," she said, her eyes wide.

"We did, too," I said, hoping she didn't mind the nickname. "Were you scared?"

She nodded, her glasses slipping down her nose.

"Me, too," I admitted, "but it's over now."

I realized it wasn't over as we drove onto Bree's block—or at least as we tried to drive onto it. We only made it past two houses before police officers stopped us, trying to get us to turn around.

"My best friend lives down there," I tried to explain to the officer as I pointed toward Bree's house. My mouth dropped open in shock because there was a huge tree covering her house.

"Where's your house?" Cory asked, peering out from the backseat.

"I don't know," Bree said. It seemed like in slow motion we all unfastened our seat belts and got out of the car. Bree ignored the officer telling her she couldn't go to her house, and I followed her, ordering Cory to stay where she was. We stood in front of the tree, staring at the house Bree had known all her life.

We looked at each other, not knowing what to say. Finally, Bree asked the question I had been thinking but dreading. "Where's my momma?"

We gazed at the house, hoping she would miraculously appear, and it seemed our prayers were answered when a woman walked from next door. It took Bree a few seconds to realize it was her neighbor. We ran over to her.

"Where's my momma?" Bree asked.

The woman hesitated. "I don't know. I saw her pulling into the driveway right before the tornado headed toward us."

"She was off today," Bree said, starting to get frantic. "She said she was going to relax."

Her neighbor frowned, then without another word, she turned and walked over to one of the officers. We watched as what seemed like hundreds of emergency personnel swarmed the area around Bree's house. I guess one of Daddy's old coworkers recognized me, because out of nowhere Daddy seemed to appear, and I knew Bree's neighborhood wasn't the area he normally patrolled. When I saw Cory next to him, I breathed a sigh of relief. In all the craziness, I had lost track of her—truthfully I had forgotten about her as I tried to calm Bree down.

Daddy suggested we go home, and it took me a while, but I finally talked Bree into it. Nathaniel met us there, and when Bree saw him, she just lost it. I was trying to be strong for her, but really I was worried, too. What if something had happened to her mom? She was really the only family Bree had.

It was around ten that night when Daddy finally came home.

The minute he stepped through the door, I knew, and apparently Bree did, too, because she collapsed and let out a scream from the depths of her soul.

Just like that, her mother was gone.

The next few days were really a blur. Aidan had called me two days after Bree's mother died to let me know his grandma had passed away. The funeral was going to be in Atlanta the same day as Bree's mom's. Momma and I were trying to help Bree with the funeral arrangements, but Bree was in serious denial. Because the house had been badly damaged, we were having a hard time locating her mother's insurance and other information. Finally, Nathaniel suggested we contact Bree's father, Oz, and he agreed to pay for everything after we finally managed to reach him. Apparently, his record label thought we were some groupies out to get some money. The only way Oz found out was because Oz's publicist had mentioned it jokingly.

It was the saddest funeral I had ever attended, not that I had been to a lot. Nathaniel had finally convinced

Bree to go view her mother's body the night before, and I had gone with her. Bree had been hysterical, and truthfully, so was I. I think there was a part of me that believed her mom was on vacation or something and soon we would see her walk through my front door as she had done so many times before.

She wasn't coming back, though.

Bree had stood over the casket, just staring at her mother, who really didn't look like herself, crying and promising her mom she was going to finish school and make her proud. I grabbed her and held her, vowing I would always be there for her, and Nathaniel wrapped himself around us, promising the same thing.

I only remembered snippets of the actual funeral: a man singing "Order My Steps," Bree throwing herself at the casket, the rain falling just as we left the church, then the sun finally shining through as we made it to the cemetery where a bunch of people, including Andrea and members of Worth the Wait, surrounded Bree to offer their condolences.

It was as we were leaving the cemetery that I spotted Oz, Bree's father. I had never seen him in person, but he had been on television enough that I recognized him. He was shorter than I'd expected—kind of reminded me of one of those little people in that old movie *The Wizard of Oz*—so I kind of understood how he had gotten his name.

He gave Bree a hug, and I wondered if she really knew who he was. She had just been going through the motions all morning, and I was really worried about her. I stood beside her, grabbed her hand and squeezed, letting her know I was there if she needed me.

"Have you thought about what you're going to do?" Oz asked.

Bree just kind of stared at him. Finally I said, "She's going to live with us."

I hadn't really discussed this with my parents, but I figured they wouldn't mind. It would only be for a few months since we were going off to college soon—at least I hoped Bree was still planning to go after all that had happened.

Oz smiled. "You've talked to your parents about that?" he said, like he was reading my thoughts.

"No, but they won't mind."

He nodded. "I'd like for you to come out to L.A. and stay with me," he said.

I pulled Bree closer to me, getting really scared at the thought of losing her. "She has to finish school. We'll be graduating in a few months," I said.

"What are you, her bodyguard?" he joked.

"Her friend," I said. He was starting to really annoy me. Bree was really in pain, and he didn't seem to see that. "I'm her best friend. If you haven't noticed, now isn't a good time to have this conversation."

"You're right," he said. He reached into his pocket and pulled out two business cards and an envelope, handing the envelope and one card to Bree and the other to me. "Give me a call whenever you're ready. There's a check in there that should help with any of your mother's expenses and anything you need." He looked at me. "Where are your parents? I need to talk to them."

I pointed them out and he walked away with his bodyguard shielding him with an umbrella since it was raining again. Oz stepped carefully over the puddles. He spoke with my parents for a minute, handed them something that looked like a check, glanced back at Bree then left.

"What are you going to do?" Nathaniel asked Bree. I had been so focused on the conversation with Oz that I hadn't even realized he had walked up.

Bree stared at him as though she was seeing him for the first time. She glanced around, taking in where we were, then she collapsed. Nathaniel caught her just before she hit the ground and carried her to the limousine. I climbed in with them, wrapping Bree in my arms as she broke down again.

"We're going to get through this," he said, kissing her and smoothing her hair.

I prayed what he was saying was true.

The next couple of months just kind of dragged past. Before I knew it, it was April, and the purity conference was three days away. Bree had been staying with us, and not a whole lot had changed. She was still missing her mom and not sure what she wanted to do about the future. She had talked to Oz once, but the conversation was short. She didn't tell me what they talked about, and I didn't ask.

Momma was huge. She was due on the day of my graduation, and I was praying she wouldn't go into labor on the biggest day of my life.

Daddy was still acting strange, disappearing and coming in late without explanations. Momma didn't seem that concerned, but I was. I had tried talking to him again, and for a minute I thought he was going to admit he had been cheating, but instead he walked off.

Aidan and I talked during school every day, but that was about it. We had both been so busy we really hadn't had time. I realized I missed him, though, and I promised myself after he came to the purity ball to see Nadia perform, we were going to get back on track. I had decided I was going to stop hiding the fact that I was dating him from my parents because he hadn't done anything wrong, and he shouldn't have to pay for what Allen had done to me. Since he and his family were still planning on coming to the purity ball, I figured that would be a good time to introduce everyone. If it was up to me, Aidan and I were going to be spending a lot of time together, so everyone might as well get used to it.

At our last planning meeting before the conference, I guess I was kind of quiet.

"You okay?" Jennifer asked.

"I guess," I said. Truthfully, I didn't know how to feel about much of anything anymore. A lot had happened to me in the last year, and since Bree had lost her mom and her baby, it really had me thinking about how important family was. I thought of Bree and smiled. As far as I was concerned, she was family, too.

"I guess I'm just realizing how much I appreciate my family—most of them, anyway," I said. The thought of Daddy seeing someone else entered my mind, but I pushed it away. I hadn't told anyone, but I had been out a few days earlier, and I had seen him from a distance with another woman. They were holding hands and laughing. Finally I had to turn away when he leaned over and kissed her. I was going to tell Momma, but I didn't know when.

"Family is important," Andrea said. I had been so lost in my thoughts I didn't even realize she had come in. She had moved to Atlanta with her fiancé, Justin, but, as she had promised, she was back for the conference. "I think one thing we can take away from Bree's mother dying is if you love someone, tell them. You never know when tomorrow might be too late."

"Yeah," Jennifer said. "We get so caught up in trying to find guys to love that we forget about the people who are there for us even when we don't have men."

Felicity laughed. "Y'all need to stop. All this sappiness is getting on my nerves. I don't know why you're feeling all warm and fuzzy because Bree's mother died. People die every day. Get over it."

I wanted to punch her for being insensitive, but truthfully I wasn't surprised. When she pulled back her sleeve to scratch an itch, I couldn't help but stare. There was a huge bruise on her wrist, and I wondered if Allen had done it. When she saw me looking, she quickly snatched down her sleeve and glanced at the floor, and I knew I was right.

"So is everybody ready for the conference?" Andrea asked. I wondered if she had seen the bruise, too, although her expression didn't change.

There were a few muttered responses. We went over our master checklist and realized somehow we had managed to get everything done ahead of schedule.

"Are you sure the news stations are going to be here?" someone asked.

"I checked with them the other day myself," I said. "You know they have been making such a big deal of it that it would have to be something major for them to miss it."

"Is Bree coming?" Jennifer asked.

"She said she was."

"I hate that she decided not to participate," Andrea said, "but I understand."

"She's going to like the fact we're dedicating the night to her mom," I said. I had been saving that as a surprise for Bree, and I knew she would be really touched.

"So that's it?" Andrea asked.

"Yes," we said in unison.

"Good. I have something for you guys." She pulled out a shopping bag filled with tiny boxes, and a few girls refused to take them at first, remembering last year when Andrea had done something similar.

"Are you giving us HIV again?" someone joked.

Most of us laughed nervously, although I'm sure there were a lot of girls wondering if that's what she was doing. I know I was.

"What are you talking about?" Felicity asked, shaking her present to see if she could figure out what was inside.

After one of the girls explained that last year Andrea had given each of us a box containing a slip of paper that informed us we had been given the gift of either HIV or AIDS, Felicity dropped the gift like it was hot.

"I'm glad to see you still remember my lesson," she said. "This is something different, I promise."

Since I was chapter president, I decided I would be the first to open my gift. Inside was a silver pendant with the words *Worth the Wait* engraved on a circular medallion with a small diamond.

"It's beautiful," I said, taking the necklace out of the box and putting it on. I grabbed a mirror out of my purse so I could admire it. "Thanks, Andrea."

"You're welcome," she said, giving me a hug. "I got one for Bree, too." She handed me another box, which I put in my purse.

After she was done giving everyone hugs, she suggested we say a prayer, which we did, asking God to make our event successful and drama-free.

I was so busy running around the day of the conference, I didn't have a chance to enjoy any of it or to sit in on any of the sessions. We had workshops for parents, young adults and preteens as well as performances by some of Birmingham's local talent. Everyone seemed to be excited, and we received a lot of compliments from parents and kids.

By the time I got home, I was exhausted, but I didn't have time to sit down because I had to get ready for the ball, which was being held that evening. A lot of people had bought tickets during the conference, and we had sold out, which I wasn't expecting.

"Next time, we're not having the ball the same night," I muttered to Bree as I put on a pearl earring. "I'm exhausted."

"You guys did a good job," she said. "I really enjoyed the sessions I attended." For the first time in months, she looked happy, and she reminded me of the old Bree, although a part of me realized after all she'd been through, she would never be the same. "Did you see those girls for the Tuscaloosa Worth the Wait chapter who showed up?"

"They have a Worth the Wait chapter at Bama?" I said absently as I focused on getting my hair right.

"Look at you, already sounding like a student there," she teased. "It's not at the school. One of the churches started a chapter."

I thought about the people I had seen at the conference that day, and suddenly I recalled a group of girls who had been wearing what looked like pink-and-white sorority paraphernalia. The more I thought about it, the more I realized I had seen WTW, which I assumed meant Worth the Wait, across the front.

I laughed. Although I loved Worth the Wait, pretending it was a sorority wasn't that serious, especially since I had already decided I was going to pledge Alpha Kappa Alpha as soon as I got a chance.

Bree laughed, too, and I smiled. "Are you excited about starting in the fall?" she asked.

I had finally made up my mind that University of Alabama was where I wanted to go. It didn't hurt matters that it was the only place I had applied, and, luckily, I had been accepted.

"Yeah," I said. "Are you?"

She hesitated. "Don't get mad at me..." she began.

I stopped the comb in midair. "What?" I said, but I knew.

"I've decided not to go to Bama," she said.

"Where are you going?" I asked.

"I haven't figured it out yet," she said. "I just need some time to clear my head, you know? Nathaniel's going to go to UAB, so maybe I'll stick around here if your parents let me, or maybe I'll go see my dad."

"Nathaniel's good for you," I said.

"I know," she said, "and Aidan's good for you."

"I know that," I said.

"Do you?" she challenged.

"Yes," I said, but I wasn't so sure.

"Aidan isn't Allen, Courtland. He's a good guy, and he really does love you."

For some reason, I needed to hear her say that. I realized there was a part of me that was scared to allow myself to love and be loved by Aidan. What if I ended up getting hurt again?

"Aidan's not perfect, Courtland," she said, reading my thoughts. "He might hurt you, but I really don't think he would do it on purpose. He's human, just like you. You might be the one to hurt him."

"I'm scared," I admitted.

"So am I," she said. "I don't know how I'm going to get through life without my mom. It was bad enough losing the baby." She paused and took a deep breath. "My mom was the only family I had."

"No, she's not," I said. "You've got me and my family. You know we've got you. You know Nathaniel has got you, too. I'm sure your dad will have your back, as well."

"I don't really know if he wants to see me. He mentioned it when we talked."

"He said it at the funeral, too. I think he means it. Why don't you give him a chance?"

"I'll give him a chance if you give your dad a chance."

I sucked my teeth and turned back to look in the mirror. "He's cheating on my mom, Bree. I can't forgive that. He's been around here and at rehearsal pretending he isn't doing anything, but I saw him."

"Maybe there's a good explanation," she said.

I whirled around to look at her. "Bree, I saw him kissing another woman. What explanation could there be for that?"

She opened her mouth then closed it. "I'm sorry," she said.

"It's not your fault. What's this going to do to my mom?" I asked. "I don't even know what to say to her."

"Maybe she already knows."

"She can't know," I said. "Why would she still be with him if he's cheating on her?"

She shrugged. "You stayed with Allen after he cheated on you, and the two of you weren't married."

She had a good point.

We finished getting dressed in silence. Once we were done, we stood looking at ourselves in the mirror. I had on a white off-the-shoulder ball gown with a full skirt and a tiara. I really did feel like a fairy princess on her way to the ball. I wondered if I would feel the same way in a few weeks when I went to the prom. Aidan and I were planning on going together, although I had been telling Momma I was going to just tag along with Bree and Nathaniel. I was going to fix that tonight, too.

Since Bree wasn't going to participate in the ceremony, she had decided to wear an off-white formal. She looked amazing.

"Look at us," I teased. "We're grown now."

We looked at each other in the mirror and grinned before Bree ran to get her camera. She snapped a picture of us, heads tilted together, grinning so hard I thought our faces were going to split. I knew in my heart, for the rest of my life, I would always remember that moment.

fourteen

We waited around for as long as we could for Daddy to show up to escort me to the purity ball. Finally, Momma said he would just meet us there. I was so angry I didn't have words. Momma looked worried, which made me madder. I couldn't believe I was letting her waste energy on Daddy when he was probably out with that other woman, but I didn't want my news to cause her to go into early labor.

As we pulled up at the Harbert Center in downtown Birmingham, I felt like I was at a movie premiere. The place was lit up and photographers and camera crews from all over the country were there.

"Did you expect all this?" Bree asked as we got in the long line of cars so Nathaniel could drop us off in front of the building.

"No," I said. "We got some calls from the press, but I didn't think national media would show up. I saw a microphone that had *Entertainment Tonight* on it."

Nathaniel shrugged. "That's nothing. I saw a crew from CNN."

"CNN," Momma screamed from the passenger seat. She was too big to drive, so Nathaniel had volunteered to chauffeur us. Aidan had offered, but I thought it would be best if I introduced him to my parents at the event. They would be less likely to trip if we were in a crowd when I introduced them, that was if Daddy showed up.

Momma pulled down her visor and started primping in the mirror, and Cory burst out laughing. We had convinced her to wear a dress, which she hadn't really done since Momma and Daddy's wedding, but this time she hadn't complained. She looked really cute in a white gown similar to mine. I could tell she was excited because she had her face pressed against the window and hadn't looked down at her Game Boy once. I realized she really hadn't been playing it as much lately, and I smiled, realizing she was growing up. So was I, I thought. I had started the year focused on playing basketball, but I hadn't thought about it in a long time. Part of me wondered if being with Allen had made the sport more interesting, but I shook the thought out of my head. There was no way I was going to let thoughts of Allen ruin my night.

We finally made it to the front of the line, and after we exited the car and started down the red carpet our Worth the Wait members had decided to get for the event, somehow word spread I was the president of our chapter, and I was getting stopped left and right for interviews and for pictures to be taken.

"Where's your dad?" someone shouted.

I had been trying to ignore the fact that all the girls at the purity ball who had walked the red carpet before me had been escorted by their fathers with the exception of Felicity, Angel and Yasmin, who had posed with dates.

Felicity was all over Allen, who was looking really good in a black tux. I briefly wondered why he was out in public when he was still wanted for raping the mayor of Mayfield's daughter. I decided that was his problem. I looked past him, and my heart skipped a beat.

There was Aidan, looking fine as wine, as my momma would sometimes say. He had on a black tux, too, and we couldn't take our eyes off each other. We walked toward each other as though drawn by a magnet.

Before I could make it to him, though, Allen had the nerve to come over to me.

"Hey, Courtland," he said.

"Hey," I said, barely making eye contact with him as I stepped around him toward Aidan.

Allen grabbed me and I flinched. It reminded me of the times before when he had put his hands on me. Aidan must have seen the fear in my eyes, because he stepped between us.

"Don't touch her," Aidan said. He didn't even wait for Allen to respond before he turned to me. "Are you okay?"

I nodded, not believing Allen was trying to ruin my night.

"Courtland, I need to talk to you for a minute," Allen said.

"We don't have anything to say to each other," I said, not even bothering to look at him. "Let's go, Aidan."

I grabbed Aidan's hand, and smiled at the way his touch made me feel.

"So it's like that?" Allen asked, throwing his arms up in disbelief.

I turned to face him, looking him dead in the eye, wanting him to know just how serious I was. "Yeah, Allen, it is. Not only did you try to rape me, you put your hands on me. You are a sorry excuse for a man, and if I never saw you again, that would be too soon."

Felicity was standing there looking stupid. "You need to watch the company you keep," I said, reaching for Aidan's hand again.

"You're one to talk," Allen said. "You want to spend your time with Mr. Worth the Wait here, and he's not even who you think he is."

"Whatever, Allen. You think your words have me scared, but they don't. You don't get to bully me anymore. I love myself too much to deal with you."

"I guess you love him, too," Allen said, laughing.

Without blinking an eye, I said, "Yeah, I do, and unlike you, he loves me, too."

For some reason, Allen found this really funny. I didn't even have the desire to find out why. Without another word, Aidan and I headed into the Harbert Center, which had been decorated beautifully. I took in the white lights that were strung all over the ballroom and it just seemed to be magic.

"You look amazing, Courtland," Aidan said. He gave me a sweet kiss on the cheek, and I blushed.

"Thank you. So do you," I said. In the distance, I saw Bree, Nathaniel, Momma and Cory approaching. "I have someone I want you to meet." I grabbed his hand again and we walked over to them.

"Momma," I said, "this is Aidan Calhoun, my boy-friend."

She looked at me and looked back at Aidan, then sighed. "It's nice to see you again, Aidan," Momma finally said.

"You, too, ma'am." Aidan shook her hand. "I apolo-gize again about my first impression. I've wanted to come over and apologize, but Courtland told me it wasn't a good idea." He laughed nervously, and he had never looked more adorable.

"It probably wasn't," Momma agreed.

"I hope we can start over. I really would like for you to get to know me. My family thinks I'm a pretty decent guy."

"So do we," Bree said, speaking for her and Nathan-iel, and I smiled my thanks.

"You're cute," Cory said and blushed. I looked at her in surprise, and she looked back at me innocently. "Well, he is," she said.

"Yeah, he is," I said. It was Aidan's turn to blush.

"Courtland," Jennifer said, interrupting our conversation, "we really need to get in place. We're about to start."

"Okay," I said. "Where's Daddy?" I looked around.

Momma frowned. "He should have been here by now. When I talked to him a few minutes ago, he said he was a few blocks away."

I decided once again to hide my disgust. "Where are Nya and your parents?" I asked Aidan. "I thought you said they were coming." I had really been looking forward to meeting his little sister, who was close to my sister Cory's age. I was hoping they would become friends.

"I came with Nadia because I wanted to see you before things got started. My mom and Nya should be here any minute. My dad will be late."

"We'll save them seats," Momma said, and I smiled. She looked at me and winked, and I knew everything was going to be all right. "Go," she said, and I scurried off.

In the dressing area, girls were doing last-minute touch-ups to their hair and makeup. A few were going through the opening dance routine while the fathers sat off to the side just chilling.

Everyone's father but mine.

I sat down in disgust, wondering what I was going to do if he didn't show up. I waited about five minutes then decided I was going to get my granddaddy, who I knew would be there by then.

I spotted him sitting next to my mother just like I knew he would be, then I frowned when I saw the woman sitting next to him. It was the woman I had seen my father kiss. She leaned over my granddaddy and said something to Momma, who laughed and said something back. I just stared at them, not believing what I was seeing.

I was just about to storm over and demand an explanation when someone grabbed my arm.

"Baby, I'm sorry I'm late," Daddy said.

I swung on him, not believing he had the nerve not only to bring his other woman with him but to have her sitting at the table with Momma, who obviously had no clue.

The whole situation just made me snap.

"How could you?" I screamed. I don't think I had ever been that angry in my life.

"I know," Daddy said, "but I promise I have a good explanation."

"You have a good explanation for bringing that woman here?" I just shook my head. The sight of him was making me sick to my stomach.

"What?" Daddy said, looking confused.

"Don't play dumb, Daddy," I screamed. "I saw her. You have her sitting at the same table as Momma. How could you?"

Before Daddy could speak, we were told it was time for our entrance. He turned to me. "I don't know what you think you saw, but I told you, I am not cheating on your mother."

"Whatever, Daddy," I said. I was trying to pretend I didn't care, but really I was fighting back tears. I couldn't believe my daddy was ruining what was supposed to be the best night of my life. I walked off but then twirled around, not able to let it go. "We're about to take a pledge for both of us to lead pure lives, and you bring that woman here. If you're not going to honor your commitment, why should I?"

He looked like I had slapped him. Before we could say anything else, we were pushed into the corridor we had to walk down to get to the dance floor. Daddy didn't say anything, and neither did I. When we finally made it to the floor, he took my hand just like we had practiced, and I curtsied to him, knowing I probably looked crazy since I'm sure my emotions showed all over my face. It took me a minute to adjust to the spotlight and the glare of the lights from the news cameras, but when I did, I realized the place was packed. I tried looking for my family. Although I knew where they were sitting, being on the dance floor had thrown off my sense of direction. I focused on getting through the dance, looking over Daddy's shoulder rather than at him like a lot of the girls were doing to their fathers.

We were about halfway through the song when there was a commotion on the dance floor. Since Daddy and I were in the middle of a circle with four other couples, it took me a minute to see what was going on, and when I did, my mouth dropped open.

Aidan, Nadia and a girl I assumed was their sister Nya were headed toward us, followed closely by Daddy's other woman, and they didn't look too happy. Before they could actually get to us, a few of the dads on the floor stopped them. I looked at Aidan, silently asking what he was doing, but it was like he didn't even see me. He couldn't take his eyes off my daddy. I looked between the two of them, wondering if they knew each other since they had never met.

"Daddy?" Nya said, looking at my daddy.

"Daddy?" I repeated, trying to figure out what she was talking about. Suddenly I felt sick to my stomach, not believing what I was thinking.

Were Aidan and Nadia my brother and sister?

I turned to Daddy, wondering if he could read my thoughts. He stood there looking just as confused as me. "Do I know you?" he finally asked. He looked from Aidan to Nadia then to the woman who was standing behind them, looking at us all in shock.

Momma waddled up, followed by Cory.

"Corwin, what's going on?" she asked when she finally got to us.

"I don't know," he said.

I didn't believe a word he said, and I was sick of his lying.

I walked over to Aidan and Nadia. "Is my daddy your daddy?" I asked.

Aidan just gave me a puzzled look.

fifteen

MY heart dropped out of my chest as I stood staring back and forth between Daddy and Aidan, not believing what was happening. My boyfriend was my brother?

In slow motion, like I was standing outside myself, I saw myself collapsing to the floor and my daddy—Aidan's daddy—catching me. There was a quiet murmur running through the room, and I knew the news cameras were filming and people were talking about us. If I weren't in the situation, I would be talking, too.

"How could you?" I screamed at Daddy once I had sat up.

"Baby, I didn't do anything," he said. "I would never hurt you, your mother or your sister. I told you that."

"What about my other brother and sisters?" I asked sarcastically. "How long have you been cheating?" I didn't even wait for him to respond. "Is that why it took you so long to marry Momma, because you had this woman on the side?"

I couldn't believe I was putting all our business out there, but really I didn't care. Nothing I said could be worse than what Daddy had done.

Suddenly, I wondered if Aidan had known we had the same daddy all along and if this was his idea of some stupid joke, like the one Allen had played on me when he started dating me because of a ten-dollar bet.

"Did you know about this?" I turned to him and demanded.

He opened his mouth to speak, but I cut him off. "You had to have known. You've been to my house...." Suddenly the tears came, and as much as I wanted to, I couldn't stop them. I couldn't believe I had been stupid enough to fall for a guy again who only saw me as a joke.

To make matters worse, Allen was standing there laughing like he had never seen anything so funny. Suddenly his comments when Aidan and I had walked into the Harbert Center made sense. He had known what was going on. I lunged at him, ready to hurt him the way he kept on hurting me. What had I done to make him hate me so much?

I had almost made it to him, but the cops got to him first and dragged him away. I rushed at him, ready to spit on him like he'd spit on me the first day of school.

"He's not worth it," the woman said. It took me a second to realize she was the woman I saw Daddy with.

I jerked my arm away and glared at her for putting her hands on me.

She wasn't even focused on Allen. "I think I know what's going on," she said softly, looking at Daddy and smiling.

I couldn't believe what I was seeing.

"I'll bet you do," I muttered, ignoring Allen's screams as he was led away. Momma was standing there, still trying to figure out what was going on.

The woman turned to Momma. "Mrs. Murphy, I promise you whatever your daughter thinks isn't true. I'm a happily married woman, and from the looks of it, so are you." She turned to Daddy. "Do you know Durwin Calhoun?"

He frowned and shook his head. It took me a second to realize I had heard the name before. Aidan had told me that was his father's name.

"No," Daddy said, looking at Momma to see if she knew the name.

She gave a slight shake of her head.

"Forgive me for being personal, Mr. Murphy," Aidan's mom said, "but were you by any chance adopted?"

"Yes," Daddy said.

I was trying to figure out where she was going with all her questions when the answer appeared right before my eyes—literally. There standing in front of me was Daddy, but this man wasn't my daddy, although he looked exactly like him. My eyes got huge as I realized my daddy had an identical twin.

Daddy saw me staring and looked over, and his eyes

got bigger than mine. There were a couple of people glancing around in confusion, Momma, Cory, Aidan, Nadia and Nya included.

I turned to Aidan, who was still staring back and forth between our daddies. "Did you know about this?" I asked again, but I could look at him and tell he didn't.

He shook his head. "This is nuts," he said in amazement.

"Yeah," I said. "Why didn't we know this? You came to my house a couple of times."

"But I never came in—well, no farther than the entryway," he said.

I thought about the times he had come over and realized he was right.

"Well, at least you're not brother and sister," Bree said, trying to find the bright spot in a crazy situation.

"So what, that makes you cousins?" Nathaniel asked, and Bree elbowed him in the ribs.

I nodded sadly. Brother or cousin, it really didn't matter. The fact was, Aidan and I were still related. I felt like I was going to throw up in my mouth. I had kissed him—a few times.

Aidan must have read my mind. "We're not really related," he said quietly.

I looked at him, not sure if I could take any more news.

"What are you talking about?" I said. "Our dads are brothers—identical twins."

"I'm Nadia and Aidan's stepfather," Durwin said. It was the first time I had heard him speak, and if I closed my eyes, I would think it was Daddy talking. I laughed.

If I *opened* my eyes, I would think it was Daddy talking. This was still incredible. How could Daddy have a brother—an identical twin brother—and no one know? I tried to focus on what Durwin—was I supposed to call him Uncle Durwin?—had just said.

"Their stepfather?" I said. "You don't have to say that to make me feel better. Aidan talks about you all the time, and he's never mentioned anything about you being his stepfather."

"That's because he is my father," Aidan said. "He might not be biologically, but he and my mom have been married since Nadia and I were three, and he's the only father I've ever known. That other guy was just a sperm donor." I had never seen him look so disgusted.

I had a lot of questions running through my mind. I wanted to ask what had happened between Aidan's mother and his real father. More than that, I wanted to know what all this meant for our relationship. A camera flash caught my attention, reminding me our whole family drama was being played out for all the world to see, thanks to the media. I groaned, not believing this was happening to me.

Since Momma had told me she was pregnant, I had accepted our family getting larger, but suddenly all these new members had my head swimming. I felt like I was walking through mud, and the room got so hot, I started having trouble breathing. I guess I wasn't looking too great, because, through hazy eyes, I saw Aidan looking at me and someone grabbed my hand.

"Courtland, are you okay?" someone said in slow motion.

I tried to nod, but it took my whole body to do it.

"Courtland," I heard Momma yell just before everything went black.

I awoke with a start from the craziest dream I had ever had in my life. I slipped on some ready-to-roll clothes—as Momma called them—a pair of sweats I could sleep in and wear outside over my panties and bra, thinking I had to be really tired to go to sleep in just my underwear, then headed downstairs when I realized Bree wasn't in my room. I knew she would find the dream just as crazy as I did.

I walked into the living room, and it took me a second to process what I was seeing. Daddy was on the sofa looking through a photo album, pointing and shaking his head at something he saw.

I looked around the room, and Aidan, Nadia and Nya were there along with the woman from my dream who had said she was their mother. Her presence scared me, and I pinched myself, wondering if I was still dreaming. I took in the television, which was airing a scene from my dream, and I started to get scared.

It wasn't until my gaze landed on Daddy again—or was it his twin?—that I realized I had awakened from a dream only to walk into a nightmare.

"I wasn't dreaming?" I said, but I must not have said it loud enough, because no one responded.

Cory bounded in from the kitchen and, spotting me, ran right over. "Daddy's family is here, and Momma's fixing a snack. You and Aidan can't go together anymore because you're cousins," she said, then skipped away like she had just announced we were going to the McWane Science Center.

I felt myself getting sick all over again, but before I could go down, Aidan rushed over to me.

"We'll work this out," he said after he'd made sure I was okay.

"How?" I asked. "We're related."

"No, we're not," he insisted.

"Yes, we are," I said, just as insistent. "You said yourself that even though your dad isn't your dad biologically, he raised you."

He didn't say anything, but I knew he agreed with me.

"This is horrible," I said. "Why can't I just have a decent relationship? I just want someone to love me."

Aidan grabbed my hand and pulled me into the entryway. "Courtland, I love you," he said. "That's not going to change. We're going to figure this out. Do you trust me?"

I looked down at the floor and nodded. He grabbed my chin and forced me to look at him. "Do you trust me?"

"Yeah, I trust you," I whispered, realizing I did. Since the first day of school, Aidan had had my back, and I had to believe he would have it this time, too.

He leaned over to kiss me, and I was just about to kiss him back when I realized as much as I loved him, he was my cousin—sort of. At the last minute, I moved my head, and his kiss landed on my cheek.

"I'm sorry," I said when I looked at him and saw the disappointment in his eyes. "This is weird for me now."

He nodded in understanding, although I wasn't sure if he really did understand.

"I just need some time to think," I said. "I'm not trying to hurt you, but one thing I learned from Allen is I've got to love myself and listen to my heart, and right now it's telling me this isn't right. Maybe I'll change my mind after I give it some thought, but right now, it's best we're just friends."

I tried to stop the tears from falling, but one slipped out anyway, and when I looked into Aidan's eyes, I saw he was on the verge of tears, too. Seeing him hurt made me hurt even more.

I couldn't stop myself from grabbing him and holding on to him with everything I had in me. He grabbed me back and held on just as tight, and we stood there just rocking and crying, trying to understand what all that had happened really meant for us.

sixteen

A month later, I still didn't have any answers about what the future held for Aidan and me. For the first couple of weeks, I saw him every day between school and his family coming over to see mine, but then it kind of slacked off. Bree told me that Aidan had skipped the prom just like me. Two days before graduation, I was thinking about skipping that, too, but I knew how important it was to my family.

My daddy had finally admitted to me the real reason he had been missing in action for the last few months. He had been finishing up his undergraduate degree so he could apply for a job in the police department's investigation division.

I didn't believe him at first, wondering why he had to keep that a secret, but he had explained he wanted to keep it to himself until he actually found out if he was going to graduate, which he was scheduled to do the weekend after me.

I headed to school with Bree and Nathaniel two days

before graduation to pick up my cap and gown, not really feeling it.

"You okay?" Bree asked on the drive to school.

"Yeah," I said, but really I wasn't. I sighed and stared out the car window, wondering how my life had gotten so crazy. Aidan was the kind of guy I had always wanted, and although part of me knew it was wrong to still be thinking about him, I really couldn't help it. How was I just supposed to shut off my feelings?

"It's going to be okay," Bree said.

I smiled my thanks, knowing she was just saying it to make me feel better.

"Can you believe this time next week we'll be high-school graduates?" Nathaniel asked.

"I know," Bree said. Suddenly she sounded a little sad, and I knew she was thinking of her mom. Nathaniel must have realized it, too, because he reached over, grabbed her hand and kissed it.

"Hey, what are we doing after graduation?" I asked. Really I didn't feel like doing anything, but I was trying to cheer Bree up.

"We can get a room," Nathaniel said.

"Uh, no," I said, and he and Bree laughed.

"I didn't mean it like that," Nathaniel said. "Bree and I have decided to be celibate until we get married." They looked at each other and smiled.

"When did that happen?" I asked.

"After the baby," she said. She didn't sound as sad when she said it as she normally did. "We love each other, and we've decided we're worth the wait." She looked back at me, knowing what I was thinking. "That was kind of corny, huh?"

"Yeah, it was," I said. "I get it, though." We grew quiet. "You think Aidan's going to be here?"

"Probably," Bree said. Nathaniel elbowed her, but she ignored him. "You know Aidan is hurting just as much as you are, Courtland."

"You think so? A part of me feels like this is the same thing that happened with Allen, like I'm the punch line in someone's joke."

"You know Aidan's not like that," she said. "He's never given you any reason not to trust him."

"Yeah, I know," I said. "How is it neither of us realized we were related?"

"I'm sure you're not the first people this has happened to," Nathaniel said. "My momma and I were talking about this—"

"You told your mother?" I said, covering my face in embarrassment.

"Uh, Courtland, it's not like it's a secret. The story about your dad and your uncle was all over the news. It got more coverage than the purity conference," Nathaniel said. "People who knew you and Aidan were dating figured out what was going on."

I groaned. "People have been talking about me again?" I asked.

"I don't know," Bree said, "but so what if they have? It's not your fault."

"Yeah, like I was saying," Nathaniel said, "my momma was saying that there are probably more relatives dating than we realize because families are so spread out now, and how often do you go to a family reunion to know who members of your family are? Plus, with all the adoptions and stuff that happen, people may not even know their biological family."

I thought about what Nathaniel was saying and realized he was right. I couldn't think of the last time I had attended a family reunion, and for all I knew I could walk past my cousin on the street and not know him. I laughed. I had been dating my cousin and didn't know him.

"Man, this is some reality-TV stuff," I said, and we all burst out laughing. "This has been a crazy year. I date an abusive guy, then I meet a great guy and I can't date him because he's my cousin. I hope college doesn't have this much drama." I put my hand on Bree's shoulder. "I still wish you were coming."

"We'll see," she said.

I didn't push her. We were making progress with her responses, so I decided to just keep praying about it and hope God would work on her heart so she would end up at the University of Alabama with me in the fall.

By the time we made it to school, it was packed. Somehow I got separated from Bree and Nathaniel, and I decided it would be a good time to clean out my locker, which I had put off doing. I guess it made the fact that I was graduating too real.

I headed to my locker, thinking of all the times I had spent at Grover over the last four years. I thought about the first time I had met Bree and all the hours we had spent talking to each other about making the cheerleading squad, not making the basketball team, meeting Allen, realizing Allen had spread the rumor that I had slept with him, meeting Aidan, all the bad things Allen and his friends had done to me, the tornado that had resulted in Bree losing her mother. Now it was all coming to an end.

A large part of my life had been spent within these four walls, and I had learned so many lessons that had nothing to do with the subjects I had been studying. I had begun my journey to loving myself, and although I was starting to realize it wouldn't happen overnight, I knew I had made huge steps. I also knew a large part of loving myself included loving my family, which was so much bigger than the people who lived in the house with me. I looked at Bree, who was heading down the hall toward me, and I knew she was my sister—we were girls for life.

"How come you're not answering your phone?" she asked, frowning at me.

"I didn't hear it ringing," I said. I grabbed my purse from the shelf where I had placed it and dug through it. "I must have left it—"

"Forget about it," she said, grabbing my arm. "Come on."

"Where are we going?" I asked. I barely had time to grab my purse.

"Your mom's in labor," she said.

"What?" I screamed and started running for the door. Momma had been complaining about her back hurting when we left that morning, but I was hoping the babies would wait until after graduation.

We ran to the car and Nathaniel was already inside. "Let's go," I said.

"I'm trying," Nathaniel muttered, turning the key in the ignition. The car coughed and sounded like it was going to start, but then it died.

"Are you serious?" I said, more to Nathaniel's old clunker than to Nathaniel.

"Come on," Bree coaxed, used to the car being temperamental.

We tried for another ten minutes, but still the car wouldn't start.

All I could think of was Momma having the babies without me being there. I spotted Aidan's car in the parking lot and ran inside to find him.

Lucky for me, he was near the office talking to the basketball coach and a few players.

"Aidan," I said, barely able to catch my breath. I bent over trying to get in enough air to speak.

"There's your cousin," one of the players said. A few of them laughed, but they stopped when Coach shot them a look. I didn't even acknowledge them.

"Momma...babies," I managed to get out, promising myself I was going to start getting back in shape, which hadn't been a priority since I had stopped playing ball.

"Baby momma. You got your cousin pregnant?"

Coach couldn't stop the laughter that time.

Aidan looked at them. "Did you say something?" he asked, and although they didn't stop laughing, they didn't say anything else. He turned to me. "Are you okay?"

I nodded. Having finally caught my breath, I said, "My momma's having the babies. Nathaniel's car isn't working. Can you take me?"

He didn't respond, instead grabbing my hand. We ran to the car.

"Can I use your phone?" I asked.

I called Daddy, but he didn't answer his phone, so I called Momma's phone and was surprised when I got an answer.

"Hello," someone said.

I frowned, trying to place the voice. "Aunt Dani?" I finally said.

"Corky, is that you?"

I didn't even bother to say anything about her using my old nickname. "What are you doing with Momma's phone? What are you doing in Birmingham?"

"I came for your graduation," she said. "I was at Daddy's when they called and said your momma was in labor, so Miles and I headed over."

"How's Momma?" I asked, not knowing how I felt about her being in town.

"Girl, she's in pain," she said.

In the background, I heard a scream so loud I had to take the phone away from my ear. "Is that Momma?" I asked.

"Girl, yes."

"We'll be there in a minute," I said. I looked at Aidan and he nodded, indicating we were almost there.

The car had barely pulled into the parking lot before I was out of it running into the hospital. Luckily Momma had dragged me along when she did the hospital tour, so I remembered exactly where to go. It didn't take long for me to find Momma's room because we had so much family hanging around it.

I threw up a hand to wave at them, then rushed into the room. Momma was looking much calmer than she had sounded on the phone.

"How are you?" I asked, taking Momma's hand.

"Much better now that I've had an epidural," she said.

I looked at her in surprise, knowing she had been against getting one. She had said she had had one with me and Cory, but she was determined to do natural childbirth with the twins.

"I forgot how bad the pain was," she said, smiling an apology.

I shrugged. I figured if they had something to take away the pain she might as well take advantage of it.

I had only been there about an hour when a nurse came in, checked the monitors on the baby and frowned. "I'll be right back," she said, then hurried out of the room. She returned a few minutes later with a doctor, then things started happening really fast.

"It looks like one of the babies is in distress," the doctor said. "I think it would be best to go ahead and get them out of there."

The only time I had ever seen Momma look that scared was the night last year Aunt Dani had been rushed to the hospital. Suddenly I started getting a little worried. As much as I had dreaded the thought of the babies coming, the thought of them not coming had me even more scared.

"Can I come?" I asked. Momma had told me I could be in the room when the babies were born, and I had secretly been looking forward to it. I had watched a lot of reality TV shows like *A Baby Story* that showed actual deliveries, but I figured it wouldn't compare to actually being there when it happened.

"I'm sorry," a nurse said apologetically. "Since this is surgery, only your dad will be allowed to be in the room."

"Are the babies going to be okay?" I asked.

The nurse gave me a sympathetic smile, which didn't do a lot to reassure me.

Momma was wheeled out of the room, and Daddy headed off to put on some scrubs. I headed to the University Hospital maternity waiting room where the rest of my family was gathered. I walked over to Cory—someone had gone to get her from school—and gave her a hug.

"Is Momma going to be okay?" she asked, looking worried as her glasses slipped down her nose.

"Yes," I said, not knowing if I was saying it for her or me.

I glanced around the room and realized everyone was looking a little nervous.

"We should say a prayer," my granddaddy said.

We obediently got up and joined hands, and I smiled when Aidan took mine and squeezed. "She's going to be fine," he whispered.

But will we? I found myself wondering. I shook the thought out of my head and focused on my granddaddy's prayer, adding my *Amen* to the chorus when he was done.

"Corky." Aunt Dani came over to me.

"Hey, Aunt Dani." She reached out for a hug, and I leaned in, realizing how much I had missed her. Even though I didn't agree with a lot of the things she did, she was still family, and I decided at that moment I was going to forgive her and love her, regardless.

"I'm sorry for everything that happened," she said, surprising me.

"Me, too," I said.

"I miss you," she said.

"I miss you, too."

She hugged me again, and when she stepped back, I really looked at her, and I realized maybe she had learned from everything that had happened. I knew I had.

We didn't get a chance to talk any more because Daddy walked in.

"Is Momma okay?" Cory asked.

Daddy nodded, then a big grin filled his face. "Your momma's fine, and so are the babies."

I breathed a sigh of relief.

"What did she have?" someone yelled.

Daddy laughed. "Two boys."

I looked up in surprise. "Really?"

"Yeah," he said. He was so excited I thought he was going to start bouncing off the walls.

"Are they okay?" someone asked.

"They're great," he said. "One weighs five pounds, seven ounces and the other is five eight."

I thought that sounded okay, but I wasn't sure. "That's good, right?"

He nodded.

"Can we see them?" Cory asked. She looked just as excited as Daddy.

"The nurses needed a few minutes to clean them up."

"What are their names?" someone asked.

"Corwin Jr. and Corbin," Daddy said. "We're still working on the middle name for Corbin."

"Corwin and Corbin," I said, testing out the names. They felt right.

"Let me get back in there," Daddy said. "I don't know if they'll let everyone come into Donna's room, so I'll try and take some pictures and bring them back for you."

I suddenly couldn't wait to see the babies. I looked over at Bree, and although I could tell she was excited, there was a touch of sadness in her eyes. I knew she was thinking about her baby who would have been born around this time.

"You okay?" I asked.

She nodded and gave me a hug. "Congratulations," she said. "You're a big sister—again."

"Yeah," I said in wonder.

We sat making small talk until Daddy finally came back a couple of hours later and said we all could go back to see the babies. I don't think I had ever seen Momma look so beautiful or so happy. While most of my family rushed toward the babies who were sharing a clear bassinet under a heat lamp, I headed toward Momma.

"Congratulations," I said as she wrapped me in a big embrace.

"Thanks," she said.

"How are you feeling?"

"Tired," she said honestly. "Those boys are already wearing me out."

I laughed. "I'll come home as often as I can to help you," I said.

It was her turn to laugh. "No, you won't."

"You're probably right," I said.

"What am I going to do without you, Courtland?" she said.

"You act like I'm never coming home again," I said. "Are you kicking me out?"

"No, nothing like that. You're about to enter a new phase of your life. If I haven't told you lately, I'm proud of you. You've grown a lot over the last year."

"So have you," I said.

"Yeah, we're both learning to love ourselves." She leaned over to me. "You couldn't have stood up to your daddy about him cheating or to me about your relationship with Aidan the way you did a year ago. Don't make it a habit," she said sternly.

"Yes, ma'am," I said, giving her a salute.

We grinned at each other.

"You should go see your brothers," she said.

"I thought I should wait for the crowd to die down," I said, looking at my family, who were busy posing for pictures with the babies.

"If you wait for that, you'll be waiting," she said.

"Good point," I said.

I gave Momma a kiss then made my way through the crowd, stopping in front of the bassinet. When I gazed at my baby brothers for the first time, my breath caught. I had never seen two cuter babies in my life.

"Can I hold them?" I managed to ask Momma.

She nodded and I picked one up. As though he sensed who I was, he smiled at me, and I grinned back at him. "Hey," I said. "I'm your big sister." He squirmed a little then let out a yawn, looking bored, and popped his thumb into his mouth.

"That's Corwin," Daddy said, nodding at the baby I was holding. "You want to hold Corbin, too?"

I shifted Corwin so he was only in one arm then settled into a rocking chair someone vacated. Daddy placed Corbin in my free arm and I gazed at him, and suddenly my heart filled with love.

I repeated the same words of welcome to him I had said to Corwin, and he looked just as bored. I gave them both kisses on the forehead then sat, content just to hold them as I took in all the people in the room. By that time, Aidan's family had shown up, and I smiled as I saw Daddy and his brother wrap each other in a warm embrace, then Daddy walked over to Momma and gave her a big kiss and thanked her for giving him four beautiful children. I looked at Aunt Dani, who was being her normal crazy self, then I focused on Bree, who had lost more than I could ever imagine in a short period of time. Finally, I looked at Aidan, who sensed my gaze on him. He winked and smiled, and I smiled back, basking in the glow of being surrounded by the people I loved who loved me. It occurred to me in that moment that no matter how crazy my life got and even when I had days where I questioned whether I loved myself or the people around me, when it was all said and done, I had the love of my family and friends, and that was good enough for me.

* * * * *

QUESTIONS FOR DISCUSSION

---

1. Courtland struggled with the fact that although her relationship with Allen was over she still thought about him and had feelings for him. Talk about a time a relationship of yours ended. How long did it take you to get over the person? Did you still have feelings for the person after you broke up?

2. Allen and his friends spent a great deal of time torturing Courtland. Describe how a person's behavior changes after a relationship ends.

3. Do you think Courtland was really over Allen when she met Aidan? Why or why not? Have you ever started a new relationship when you knew you still had feelings for someone else? How did this affect your new relationship?

4. Do you think Courtland truly cared for Aidan? Why or why not?

5. What lessons, if any, do you feel Courtland learned from her relationship with Allen? What lessons have you learned from your relationships?

6. What mistakes did Courtland make in her new relationship with Aidan? What mistakes have you made in your relationships?

7. Was Courtland a good friend to Bree when Bree really needed her? Talk about a time you've had to be a true friend to someone. Do you feel you were a good friend, or did you let the person down?

8. Was Courtland right to confront her father about her suspicions? Why or why not? Have you ever had to confront your parent or another adult about something? If so, what did you say?

9. Ultimately, Courtland realized the importance of family. How important is your family to you? What are some ways you can improve the relationship or show them they are important?

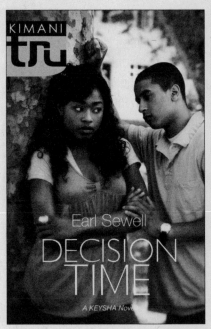

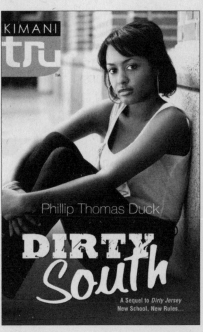

Curveball, coming right up....

Indigo Summer and her best friend Jade are the best dancers on the high-school dance team. Now one of them is going to be team captain—Indigo just never expected it to be Jade. Jealousy suddenly rocks their friendship. And they're not the only ones dealing with major drama. Their friend Tameka is destined for a top college…until one lapse in judgment with her boyfriend changes everything.

Friendships, the team, their futures…this time it's all on the line.

Coming the first week of June 2009 wherever books are sold.

DEAL WITH IT
An INDIGO Novel

ESSENCE BESTSELLING AUTHOR
Monica McKayhan

www.KimaniTRU.com
www.myspace.com/kimani_tru

KPMM141I0609TR